THE WOLF'S TREASURE

A BROOKE REYNOLDS AND MARK BUTLER STORY

BRENT TOWNS

The Wolf's Treasure
Paperback edition
Copyright © 2022 Brent Towns

Rough Edges Press
An imprint of Wolfpack Publishing
1115 N. Fort Avenue, Ste. 201
Tucson, AZ 85710

roughedgespress.com

Paperback ISBN 978-1-68549-107-9
LCCN 2022935235

ROUGH
EDGES
PRESS

The Wolf's Treasure
Paperback Edition
© Copyright 2022 Brent Towns

Rough Edges Press
An Imprint of Wolfpack Publishing
5130 S. Fort Apache Rd. 215-380
Las Vegas, NV 89148

roughedgespress.com

Paperback ISBN 978-1-68549-107-9
LCCN 2022931255

THE WOLF'S TREASURE

"We will go down in history either as the world's greatest statesmen or its worst villains."
—Hermann Göring

THE TREASURE

Rome, Italy, September 1943

A gust of chill wind laden with dust swept across the cobblestone street, blowing the SS-Oberstgruppenführer uniform of a tall blond man who stood watch over the loading of trucks by his men. Each heavily laden box required no less than two bearers to manage the weight. With the addition of each box Gerhard Wolff watched the springs on the truck sink lower and lower.

"That is enough for that truck, bring the next one," he snapped curtly.

The allotted driver moved quickly, climbing into the cab where he turned the key. The old vehicle roared to life in a cloud of black smoke, and the gearbox crunched as he put it in gear, moving it out of the way. The vacated space was quickly taken as the next one in line maneuvered into position to begin being loaded. The driver climbed down and hurried across to Wolff. He snapped a sharp salute and asked, "Where will I take this one, sir?"

"Wait until the others are ready and then I will tell you."

"Jawohl."

The driver disappeared, and once more the SS general concentrated his gaze on the front doors of the Bank of Italy, anxiously awaiting the appearance of the next box of gold from within. It had been almost two weeks since Italy had surrendered to the Allies.

Most of the gold would be trucked north into the Italian Alps where it would be sequestered away until after the war. Other gold would be hidden elsewhere with the exception of those bars destined for Hermann Göring's palatial villa, Carinhall, in the Schorfheide Forest. They would join the many other treasures collected by Göring over the course of the war.

An additional six trucks were similarly loaded as those before them. When the last chest was on board, an SS-Sturmbannführer approached Wolff. Young and blond, a product of the Hitler Youth, his name was Ernst Fischer.

"The last of the gold has been loaded, General."

"Good. You will be in the lead truck. I am relying on you, Ernst, to keep it moving."

"Jawohl. I will not fail you, Herr General."

Wolff smiled. "I am sure you won't."

"What are your orders for the extra truck?"

The SS general looked at him thoughtfully for a moment before saying, "Take it to Hohenschwangau Castle where the extra artworks are stored."

"Jawohl."

Fischer saluted and then turned away, walking back down the sandstone steps he'd ascended for his discussion with Wolff. The SS general watched him open the door then swing up into the last truck filled, maintaining his watchful position, a lonely sentinel until the trucks had gone, a cloud of diesel smoke the last vestige of evidence of their passing. Wolff turned his hard, blue-eyed gaze to the crowd of Italians standing in the street, watching the cleanout of the gold.

Halfway down the steps stood two of his sergeants, his own personal bodyguard, both big men, veterans of the Russian Front, armed with MP40s. He contemplated giving them the order to fire but then changed his mind. Instead, he walked down the steps and across to his waiting Daimler-Benz G4 Staff Car.

Once he and his men were comfortable in the rear seat, the driver smoothly moved the big vehicle onto the cobbled road, following in the wake of the heavily laden trucks in their exit from Rome.

———

Florence, Italy, August 1944

The sound of distant thunder seemed to fill the clear skies. Had there been clouds about, one could have mistaken the artillery of the British 8th Army for an actual storm. But that wasn't the case. The British were on the outskirts of Florence and pushing hard to break into the city.

The Germans had blown five of the six bridges across the Arno river already, leaving one intact for the retreat of the battered defenders of the city.

Outside the Uffizi Gallery was a line of German trucks. SS soldiers worked hard as they emptied the historic building of precious things under the watchful eye of Wolff. Most of the treasures here were to be shipped back to Berlin. Most, but not all. Hermann Göring had a detailed list of those he wanted for himself.

By the time Wolff and his men were finished, thirteen trucks were loaded with five hundred and twenty-nine paintings and one hundred and sixty-two sculptures.

Fischer said to Wolff, "The last truck is loaded with the artworks for the Reichsmarschall."

The SS General nodded. "See that he gets them. Is the ledger filled out correctly?"

"Yes, sir."

"Do not lose it and I'll see you in Germany when I arrive."

"Yes, sir."

———

Carinhall, Schorfheide Forest, January 1945

Göring wasn't happy. Everything was crashing down around him, and he felt powerless to do anything about it except remove as much as possible before all avenues of escape were closed. To the west the Americans and British were closing in; to the east, the Russians were driving the German army back miles each day.

One of the Wehrmacht soldiers dropped a crate he was loading into one of the trucks and glanced at the Reichsmarschall. "Idiot," Göring snapped. "Be careful. Do you know how valuable these things are?"

The soldier glanced again at his obese commander before picking it up and loading the crate into the rear of the truck with the other things.

"Herr Reichsmarschall, we have finished sealing the room."

Göring turned to face Wolff. "Good. Make sure the rest of it gets onto the trucks. You have good men in charge of the separate convoys?"

Wolff nodded. "I hand-picked them myself."

"And what of the other matter?"

"I received word that Königsberg Castle is almost empty."

"The room?"

"It has taken special priority. It will be aboard the ship which will finish loading tomorrow and be ready to sail in a couple of days. The submarine will leave as soon as it is loaded, and the trucks will go to Portugal as you have asked."

"Thank you, Wolff."

The man clicked his heels together and bowed. He reached inside his uniform great coat and pulled out a book the size of a large diary. "Here, sir. This is one of the ledgers you will require. The others will be delivered to you directly."

Göring took it and flicked through the pages. Everything was meticulously listed, dated, and numbered. "I will not forget this, Wolff. After the war, come and find me, I will make sure you are rewarded for your efforts."

"Thank you, Reichsmarschall."

"Where will you go, once we are done here, Gerhard?" Göring asked.

"I am to go back to Italy, sir. It is a lost cause."

The big man nodded grimly. "I'm to return to Berlin. We shall all be together when the city falls. Although I have heard Hitler say that they will never take him alive."

"He will fight?" Wolff asked.

"Pah," Göring spat. "He will find a nice quiet place in his bunker and put a bullet in his own head. That is what our illustrious leader will do."

He knew the risk of speaking like that but what did it matter now? The glorious Third Reich was doomed. It would be annihilated between two massive armies. Göring continued. "Like I said, Gerhard, survive the war. Do whatever you have to, and you will be one of the richest men alive."

"I will do my best, Reichsmarschall."

———

Danzig, West Prussia, 30th January, 1945

The day was cold and dim. Friedrich Petersen, captain of the *Wilhelm Gustloff*, stood on the deck, watching as the last of the passengers came aboard. It was called Operation Hannibal: the evacuation of troops, civilians, technicians who worked on experimental weapons, from East and West Prussia ahead of the Soviet advance.

"Kapitan?" a voice called from behind him.

Petersen turned to see one of his junior officers with a clipboard in his hand. Petersen nodded and said, "Well, Helmut, what is the final tally?"

"Approximately ten and a half thousand, sir. Including the crew."

Good grief, Petersen thought to himself. "Where are we putting them, Helmut?"

"Wherever they will fit, sir. We should be ready to sail just after midday."

"Fine, fine. Make sure everyone aboard understands that they must keep their life preservers on."

Helmut nodded. "There was something else, sir."

"Hmm?"

"The cargo that came aboard earlier this evening."

"What about it?"

"The lieutenant and his men have stayed with it. They are armed."

Petersen frowned momentarily but then dismissed it. "Let it be. I cannot be bothered with them. Especially when they were two days late. They are in storage, are they not?"

"Yes, sir."

"Then leave them there."

"Yes, sir."

Preparations continued for the next couple of hours before the *Wilhelm Gustloff* was ready to sail. Then at 12:30 pm the ship sailed from Danzig in the company of the liner *Hansa*, and two torpedo boats. By some strange coincidence, a short time later both the torpedo boat and the *Hansa* developed mechanical problems. Petersen was on the bridge when the news came through.

"Herr Kapitan, the *Hansa* is reporting some mechanical fault in her engine room. She is returning to port."

Petersen nodded, not taking his gaze off what lay beyond his ship's bow.

"That is not all, sir," Helmut said as he held up a second signal. "One of the torpedo boats is reporting problems as well. It too is turning back."

"I see. Carry on."

Late in the afternoon, the temperature dropped dramatically, and Petersen pointed the ship for deep water which he knew had been cleared of mines earlier. It was against the advice of other captains aboard the ship, but she was his to command, not theirs. As darkness settled across the sea, the ice floes came. Instead of the sea temperature being an estimated 39 degrees Fahrenheit, it was down to a deathly zero. Then word came of a minesweeping convoy. Petersen ordered his red and green navigation lights to be lit.

Not long after the *Gustloff* was sighted by the S-13, a Soviet submarine under the command of Captain Alexander Marinesko.

For two hours the submarine commander followed the two German ships before surfacing and moving in to attack the *Gustloff*. Marinesko fired three torpedoes, all of which struck the ship. One almost blew off the ship's bow, the second hit amidships. The third hit the engine room, disabling everything including communications.

As the *Gustloff* started to rapidly list, Petersen gave

the order to abandon ship. "Get all of the lifeboats into the water now," he ordered Helmut.

"But we don't have enough, sir."

"I know. Just do it. And send up flares."

It was reported that only nine lifeboats were launched. Many of the passengers and crew jumped from the listing ship. Petersen noticed that many of them didn't have their life preservers on, having removed them when it became too hot below decks. "Damn fools," he muttered to himself.

———

Below decks in the storage compartment, Lieutenant Heinrich Jager and his men were thrown suddenly to the deck, the result of the torpedo's impact with the vessel. They gathered themselves slowly before regaining their feet. Jager reached for a flashlight attached to his belt.

"What was that?" one of the young privates asked, fearful of what the answer might be.

"We have been torpedoed," their sergeant said. "I'm sure of it."

"We must get out of here," the private blurted out.

"Agreed," Jager said as he began to feel the ship start to list. "Follow me."

They walked towards the sealed hatch. Jager tried to turn the wheel to open it, but it remained fast. "Schultz, give me a hand here."

Jager passed the flashlight to the private to hold while they joined efforts in trying to force the wheel. Their grunts and groans echoed around the storage chamber as they used all their might but to no avail—it would not budge.

"Look!" the private exclaimed pointing the flashlight at the floor.

An inch of water was starting to lap around their boots. He threw himself at the hatch, dropping the flashlight in the process. Men began shouting as they fought their rising panic and turned the wheel, whooping loudly when it moved ever so slightly.

With renewed vigor the German soldiers strained harder until the wheel moved the last little bit, and the lock went all the way back.

The hatch burst inward under the immense pressure of water, the force that of an exploding bomb. The soldiers were tossed backward across the floor, like flotsam on a wave, one crashing into a pile of wooden crates. Thousands of liters of ice-cold water poured in through the opening, saturating the men as they gasped for air.

The water level rose quickly, and they were soon struggling to keep their heads above it in search of every last gulp of precious air until there was no more. The ship was flooded and there was nowhere else for them to go.

———

It took around forty minutes for the *Wilhelm Gustloff* to lay over onto its side and then sink into the frigid waters some sixteen nautical miles from port. Of the more than ten thousand passengers and crew only around 1250 survived including her captain. When she disappeared below the surface, she took with her the secret of the mysterious cargo in her storage.

1

THE LEGEND OF LAKE TOPLITZ

Lake Toplitz, Austria, Present Day

"I've found something, Brooke. Over here."

Brooke Reynolds looked up from where she was scratching at a square, moss-covered block to where her partner, Frank Butler was hunched over an even larger block.

Brooke, in her early thirties, long dark hair tied back in a ponytail, tanned face, six foot-two, athletic build. It had been two years since she had left the Global Corporation and Team Reaper, after its owner and founder was asked to help an old friend. The fact that she knew a lot about the field she was operating in helped. Then she'd been offered the job as security specialist and accepted.

She wore a white singlet top and a pair of fitted denim jeans – not so tight that she couldn't slip her Glock 19 in the back of them.

Frank Butler was in his late fifties with graying hair and a solid build. Butler worked for the Schmidt Foundation which was a German company run by a billionaire dedicated to the finding and retrieval of art and artifacts that had disappeared from countries across the globe over the course of time. The current assignment was the search for, recovery, and repatriation of treasures stolen by the Nazis during the Second World War. And the heavily scented pine forests around Lake Toplitz in Austria was rumored to be one of the caches the Nazis had utilized to stash their massive hoard.

"What do you have, Frank?" Brooke asked as she straightened up and walked towards his position.

"Come, have a look," he said eagerly.

Brooke stopped when she reached him and he pointed at something on the large moss-covered, stone block. "There, see it?"

At first, nothing was obvious, and she shook her head. Keeping her eyes fixed on the block, she let them go in and out of focus a couple of times before something materialized from everything around it. The spread wings of the eagle. The swastika. "A German Parteiadler," she murmured.

"What if the Germans never dumped their treasure into the lake?" Butler theorized. "What if all they dropped in there were boxes of rocks? What if that's all the witnesses saw?"

"It's possible, I guess."

"Then it's possible we might be looking in the right place," he told her. "Remember the notes Johann showed us? There was one place which mentioned the eagle overlooking the deep. It was thought that the large statue of the Parteiadler on the other side of the lake overlooked where the treasure had been dumped. The deepest part of the lake. What if they had it wrong? This marker is here on its own."

Brooke could see he was beginning to become excited and that in turn had her starting to feel the same way. "What are you thinking, Frank?"

"I'm thinking that it's not in the lake and this marker is exactly that. A marker."

"You think the treasure is under here?"

"That's exactly what I think."

With an eagerness afforded a young teenager he started using his bare hands to scrape away the dirt and leaves from around the marker. Within moments, he'd cleared a four-by-four-foot square of everything atop of it and was standing looking down at a concrete slab with seams around its edges. "There," he said. "What did I tell—"

THWAP!

Frank Butler stopped and stiffened. Before he'd even started to fall Brooke had already dropped to the damp foliage beneath her. Her eyes grew wide as her friend and the man she'd been assigned to protect fell beside her.

"Frank!" she exclaimed. "Frank, are you OK?"

Her protectee, however, was beyond hearing. The bullet that had hit him in the chest had killed him instantly.

"No, no, no," Brooke muttered. She scrambled on hands and knees towards a deadfall, seeking cover from the shooter.

An additional two shots smacked into the ground beside her as she moved. Managing to make the cover she drew her Glock 19. The shooter was using a suppressed weapon, possibly a sniper rifle, and all she had was her handgun.

Her emotions a tumultuous mess inside her, she tried to process what had just happened. "Get a grip, Brooke. Now is not the time. There will be a time to mourn when this is all over. If I make it."

Taking several deep breaths to calm herself, she assessed her options while getting her bearings. Out there the shooter would be changing position, trying to get a clear shot at her. Which meant that staying put for too long was as good as a death sentence. There was only one thing for it.

Brooke looked down the slope to where great granite boulders retained the hill, preventing it from sliding into the lake below. The drop from top to bottom was around fifty feet. She ground her teeth together and said in a low voice, "I'm sorry, Frank."

Brooke rose out of a crouch and blew off half her magazine, shifting her aim after each shot. Taking a deep breath, she turned and sprinted—as fast as her legs would carry her— towards the cliff. The blood rushing around her body thumped loudly in her ears as she took each stride, her compact muscles rippling beneath her clothing.

She closed the distance to the edge of the cliff quickly and for a fleeting moment thought she'd actually make it. But just as she launched herself over the edge the shooter reached out and touched her on the right side of her back, just below her shoulder blade. The force of the bullet strike thrust her forward with a violent shove. Brooke cried out and her arms windmilled wildly as she plummeted towards the murky water below.

Hitting the water hard, the air rushed from her lungs in a painful whoosh. The cloudy depths were bitterly cold, and she fought the urge to suck in a breath for fear of filling her lungs with liquid. Pain radiated from the bullet wound, her strength all but abandoning her body from being shot.

Brooke gritted her teeth, the effort of trying to claw her way back to the surface before losing consciousness sapping what power she held in reserve. Grab and pull. Grab and pull. She forced handfuls of water past herself heading for the light above her. A light that seemed to be getting dimmer and dimmer until it was suddenly extinguished.

———

On the flat-topped granite boulder at the edge of the cliff, a pair of black polished boots stood, the barrel of a suppressed DSR-Precision DSR-1sniper rifle almost brushing the top of the boots. Uttering a string of German invective, the shooter used the weapon to fire three rounds into the water below him.

The boots clicked on the hard surface of the rock as he turned around and retreated from the edge. This time his voice could be heard. *"Beide sind tot. Wir müssen den Schatz so schnell wie möglich bewegen."* Both are dead. We have to move the treasure as quickly as possible.

———

"Where am I?" Brooke asked with a groan as she came to, slowly gathering her senses to the startling realization that she was still alive.

"Meine Hütte am See," a voice replied in German. *My hut by the lake.*

Turning her head slowly, she took in the gray-haired man seated beside her bed. "I'm sorry, but who are you?"

"I am Gunther. Who are you?"

"Brooke."

The man nodded. "A beautiful name. It suits," he said sagely.

"How long have I been here?"

The man shrugged. "Three days, four."

For a moment she was confused, then, "I was shot."

"Yes, you were, but I managed to get the bullet out."

"You?" Brooke asked with surprise.

"Yes. I did not know if you wished for me to call the police," Gunther replied.

"How did you—"

The man chuckled. "I was once a medic in the German army. A long time ago."

Brooke's eyes widened. "Frank!"

The man's eyes dropped. "I am sorry, but your friend is gone."

"I know," she replied quietly. "The person who shot me shot him first."

"Yes. What were you doing to attract such attention?"

"We were looking for something."

"The lost Nazi treasures?" Gunther asked.

"Yes."

"What did you find?"

Brooke moved in the bed, trying to make herself more comfortable, and gasped as pain from her wound shot through her.

"It would be better if you remained still," Gunther cautioned her. "You do not want to burst your stitches."

"I think so," Brooke agreed, taking a breath to overcome the pain. Then she said, "We found a Parteiadler on a small block. It was a marker. My friend believed it was what we were looking for."

The German nodded knowingly. "It was only a matter of time before it was found."

Brooke was confused. "Wait, you knew it was there?"

"Yes."

"How?"

"My father."

"Your father?"

"My father was a young private in the Wehrmacht when it was put there," Gunther explained. "He was part of the party responsible for hiding it."

Brooke couldn't believe what she was hearing. "You've known it was there all this time?"

"Yes."

"Why didn't you say anything?" she asked, gob smacked.

"Because I am not the only one with the knowledge," he explained. Rising from the chair, he left the room, leaving Brooke to process what she'd just been told.

When he returned, he held out a book. "Do you read German also?"

"Yes."

"Here, my father's journal. It will explain some things."

Brooke took it. "You said there are others watching it. The ones who killed my friend?"

"Yes, that's right."

"Who are they?"

"I do not know," Gunther replied. "But your friend was not the first to die."

———

From the diary of Hans Becker:

Our orders changed not long after we left Carinhall. Instead of going to Berlin, the convoy was directed to Austria. I don't know why, or where the orders came from. It could have been the Reichsmarschall or even SS-Oberstgruppenführer Wolff. I do not know if the others had their orders changed or even if they went back for the rest of the angel's treasure.

It continued down further.

… We drove through the night until we reached the lake. Under the cover of darkness, the trucks were unloaded into the

underground bunker which had been prepared. We finished before dawn then sealed the chamber.

Not long after, I went into the trees to relieve myself. It was then I heard the gunfire.

When I went back to check, I found that all the men who had helped had been shot. The SS-Hauptsturmführer was walking around them putting final bullets into their heads. This had nothing to do with war; it was murder and greed.

I stayed hidden in the forest until after dawn. All that remained were the bodies of my comrades, left to rot in the forest. I will bury them tomorrow.

Something else I saw today was across the lake when I went down to the cliff. I saw a boat with German soldiers in it. They were dumping boxes and crates into the lake.

The place where the treasures are concealed was marked with a stone with a Parteiadler upon it. Perhaps so it can be easily identified after the war is done.

For me, the war is over. I will remain here by the lake with my comrades. I want nothing to do with what lays beneath the earth. It is bathed in blood.

2

THE FOUNDATION

Red Rock, Montana, Two Weeks Later

Taking Mark Butler's hand in his own, a gray-haired man with a heavy accent said, "I'm so very sorry for your loss. He was a great man and friend. My name is Johann Schmidt."

"Pity he couldn't have been home more," Mark said with a hint of bitterness.

The man nodded knowingly. "Yes, your father's work took him all around the world."

"His work was very important, but at times it felt like he made it more of a priority than my mother or myself," Mark growled.

The man's eyes showed his sadness at hearing the words. "I knew your father and I know for a fact that it isn't true."

"Really? Where was he when my mother died? I'll tell you; he was out of the country, chasing his dreams."

The dark-haired young man's broad shoulders slumped forward, and he turned away from Schmidt, unwilling to listen to anymore, having grown up hearing ramblings about what a great man his father was. He stared at the open grave.

Having been deployed at the time of his mother's death, Mark still harbored a multitude of guilt about his mother dying alone. He blamed his father for leaving them alone for most of the year while working on digs. But he'd turned around and followed in those size eleven shoes. Throwing himself into his studies to impress his absent father, he'd gone off to college and studied archaeology, having enough before making it about halfway through the course, joining the military for the next few years with service in Afghanistan.

"I just wanted to say that I'm sorry," the man reiterated.

He turned away and started to walk off.

"Wait."

The man turned back to see Mark facing him. "I'm sorry. You're right, it's not true. It's just—"

The man nodded. "I understand. We all need someone to blame at times."

Mark nodded. "Yes."

"*Es tut mir leid für deinen Verlust*," the man said. *I am sorry for your loss.*

"*Danke für Ihre netten Worte*," Mark replied. *Thank you for your nice words.*

Once more, the man turned and walked between the headstones, leaving Mark alone by the grave. Watching the man moving away, Mark noticed that he was soon joined by a much younger woman with long dark hair, who seemed to be moving a little stiffly. They crossed the green lawn of the cemetery and climbed into a black Mercedes SUV. As they drove off, Mark was left standing on his own beside his father's grave, wondering who they might be.

———

"What do you think?" Johann Schmidt asked Brooke as they drove away.

"He seems angry," she replied.

"I realize that," Schmidt said abruptly. "You know what I am talking about."

"He's big enough," she said with a shrug.

"You read his folder."

"Yes, mid-twenties, excels at history and his languages are exceptional. He speaks four quite fluently."

"Yes, I heard his German."

"He looks like his father," Brooke pointed out.

"I did notice that also," Schmidt agreed.

"I'm not sure whether he'll be dedicated enough. Quitting college before he had finished his degree to go into the military. Then he got out a few years into a very promising career."

"Yes but he had external studies as well."

"None of which he completed," Brooke pointed out.

"You can teach him what he needs to know."

"If he's willing to learn."

"I think it's best if we go to see him tomorrow and approach him with the proposition."

"Do I get a say in this, Johann?" Brooke asked.

The billionaire sighed. "Of course, but he was born for this."

"If, and I say only *if* he agrees, I get final say on whether he goes out into the field. The last thing I want to do is to get him killed just like his father."

"I wish that you could realize his father's death was not your fault, *meine liebste*. But I will agree to those terms."

"Thank you," Brooke said. "On both counts."

———

Mark was scratching his beer addled head when he opened the door to his hotel room, staring quizzically at the pair standing in the hallway. "What are you doing here?" he asked surprised at their appearance.

"May we come in?" Schmidt asked politely.

"What?"

"The man asked if we could come in," Brooke said abruptly.

"Who are you?"

"Just let us in and we'll tell you everything."

"Brooke, please," Schmidt admonished her. "Give the man time to process the question and reach his own conclusion."

"Why do you want to come in?" Mark asked, not taking his brown eyes from Brooke.

"I prefer to talk business in—" A door opened across the hall, and two people, a young man and woman, emerged from the room, mischief written all over their faces. After they'd walked past, Schmidt tried again, "I prefer to talk business in private, if that is all right with you?"

"OK, come in," Mark said impatiently, but allowed them to pass.

He closed the door and turned to face the strange pair, hands on hips, expecting an explanation for the intrusion. When he noticed Brooke glancing around, her nose crinkled at the state of the room, clothes everywhere, empty bottles. He said, "The cleaning lady had the day off."

She turned her green-eyed gaze on him and said, "Looks more like a month to me."

For some reason, her remarks embarrassed him. But it soon turned to anger, and he said, "You don't have to be here, lady. The door is over there."

"Before my associate gets us ejected, Mister Butler, at least give me the courtesy of hearing me out."

"All right, then, make it quick."

"As I mentioned at your father's funeral yesterday, my name is Johann Schmidt, and this is my associate Brooke Reynolds. Your father was working for me when he was killed," Schmidt said, dumping it out there like a rock in a pond.

With no response from Mark, the German kept going. "He was looking for artifacts, treasures if you like, that the Nazis stole during the Second World War. It was what got him killed in the end."

"You?" Mark asked, his face turning into a mask of anger. "He was killed because of you?"

"He was killed because he found—are you familiar with the Lake Toplitz treasure?"

"You got my father killed," Mark stated, ignoring the question, and took a step towards the German.

Brooke was quick to intervene, her right hand pressing firmly against Mark's chest. "Just hold it there, Buddy. You want to blame someone for your father's death, blame me. I was there with him."

"Brooke," Schmidt cautioned her.

"I was there to protect him," she continued. "Instead, he was killed. I failed at my job so back the fuck off."

It was a lot for the man to process, and the German billionaire could feel the situation starting to heat up. He raised his voice and spoke in German as he did when angry. "*Die einzigen Schuldigen sind die Verantwortlichen.*" *The only culprits are those responsible.*

"*Wer ist verantwortlich?*" Mark shot back at him. *Who is responsible?*

"We cannot be certain," Brooke answered. "What we do know is that we found something, but your father was killed before we could find out what."

"Found what?"

Calmer now, Schmidt continued, "As I was saying before, have you heard of the Lake Toplitz Treasure?"

"How could I not? My father's work for many years was all about recovering the treasures stolen by the Nazis."

"That is what the foundation is about. Finding lost treasures and antiquities and returning them to their rightful place."

"What foundation?"

"Mine. The Schmidt Foundation."

Mark waited for him to continue.

"As I said, your father and Brooke were at Lake Toplitz and were on the brink of a great discovery when it all happened."

"It wasn't in the lake, was it?"

Schmidt stared at him. "How did you know?"

"My father believed that the things thrown into the lake were nothing more than a ruse. He never said it out loud, but he alluded to that end."

"You're right, it wasn't in the lake."

"Did he get to see it before he died?"

The German shook his head. "No."

"We have this," Brooke said holding out a book.

Mark looked it over. "A diary?"

"Yes, one kept by a man who was an integral part of moving the treasure."

Mark took it without thinking. He opened the aged leather cover and began thumbing through the pages. When he was finished, he looked up and said quizzically, "There's a secret room at Carinhall?"

"That's what it says," Schmidt said.

"I thought most of the treasures were moved to Berchtesgaden."

"In our business there are lots of stories, theories if

you like. The hardest task we face is sorting fact from fiction."

Mark looked at the diary once more. If there was one thing he'd inherited from his father, it was his thirst for adventure. And right then, he was staring at one of the biggest.

"How does one-hundred thousand Euros sound?" Schmidt asked.

"What?"

"For every year you work for me I will pay you one-hundred thousand Euros."

Mark couldn't believe what he was hearing. "But why do you want me?"

"You are your father's son," Schmidt said. "You speak four languages, you know your history, you can take care of yourself, and you will have Brooke with you by your side."

"Brooke?" He looked at the woman before him.

She stared hard at him. "That's me if your booze addled brain hadn't worked it out."

Thinking about his aimless months since leaving the military, he said, "When do we leave?"

Schmidt smiled. "Now."

——————

Berlin, Germany, Four Days Later

The Schmidt Foundation was housed in a large structure that had served a special purpose throughout the war. It had been a blockhouse flak tower, one of the remaining few that had protected Berlin. Late in the war the flak towers had also housed some of the treasures which had been looted from numerous countries. But as the Russians began encircling the city, most of the artifacts had been removed. Those that couldn't be transferred were left behind, discovered by Soviet soldiers and lost forever.

Several years before, the German government considered knocking the structure down, wishing to eradicate many of the landmarks which constituted a reminder of the brutal regime known as The Third Reich. However, Schmidt, using some form of confidential leverage, convinced the then government to sell the tower to him to be converted into an office tower.

Now Mark, Schmidt, and the rest of his team were gathered in the conference room on the top floor, sifting through what they had been able to glean from the tragic foray to Lake Toplitz.

"Before we get started, I would like you all to meet Mark Butler, Frank's son."

Mark climbed to his feet and walked to the front of the room to take his place beside Schmidt. "Mark will be taking over his father's work."

"Is that wise?" asked a man with light colored hair.

"Mark, meet Greg Turow. He's our lead document investigator. He pores through countless documents, diaries, and letters which may or may not point us in the right direction. He also worries a lot. He was a professor at Harvard until I knocked on his door."

"Hi," Mark said with a nod.

"I'm sorry about your father," Turow said. Then to Schmidt, "We don't even know if he can take care of himself."

"Don't be so quick to judge, Greg. I'm quite sure he is more than capable."

Turow gave a stiff nod.

"Next is Molly Roberts," the German said, indicating to a young woman with pink hair and a nose ring. "She's our top electronic researcher. She's an Oxford University graduate. Her fingers are filled with electronic magic. She digs through countless files on the web which are available, for one, maybe two words which lead her to the next clue in the puzzle. She is brilliant."

She waggled her slender digits at him and said with a heavy British accent. "You need anything just shout."

"I will, thanks," Mark replied.

"Brooke you know," Schmidt said. "Werner Krause is our German Historian. More specifically from the turn of the century to the end of the war. He used to teach history, but I needed him more. Now he researches it for me."

Krause was thickset and maybe late twenties. He nodded at Mark and said, *"Willkommen im Zoo."* *Welcome to the zoo.*

"Dankeschön." *Thank you very much.*

"This is our artifact expert," Schmidt said as he walked over to a lady perhaps a little younger than Mark. She had long, dark hair that reached past her shoulders, and a fine-featured face. "Meet Isabella Pavesi. She is a fount of information upon which we all depend. She grew up in Italy and studied under the best professors where she refined her studies to artworks and artifacts."

"Ciao signorina," Mark said confidently. *Hello, Miss.*

Isabella smiled at him.

"And lastly we have Mister Webster. He's our—how should I say—"

"Hacker," Brooke interrupted quickly.

Schmidt smiled. "Yes, hacker."

"Howdy," Mark greeted him.

The young man grunted. "Yeah right."

"Where did you find him?" asked Mark.

"Jail."

Mark nodded. "Explains a lot."

"Now that you know everyone," Schmidt said, "take a seat and we'll get started."

Mark sat back down near Brooke.

"Right, what has occurred during my absence?"

"I examined the diary," said Turow, "and it appears to be legitimate."

"Of course, it is!" Brooke snapped. "I was there."

"What I mean is—never mind."

"I found a satellite that had passed over the area and managed to get some feed from it. The results were pretty dismal," Webster told Schmidt.

"What did it show you?" the German billionaire asked.

"Not a lot. There was some activity around the site, but we can assume that it was the bad guys cleaning out the vault."

"Were you able to follow them?"

"No."

"Pity."

"The Museum for National Antiquities sent a team to the lake and found nothing," Isabella reported. "It was to be expected though."

"Yes," agreed Schmidt. "Is there anything to be gained from the diary, Werner?"

"Not a lot," Krause said. "It just directs us back to Carinhall and the secret room."

"A secret room that anyone so far has failed to find," Schmidt pointed out.

"Do we have a map of the Carinhall grounds?" Mark asked, his interest piqued.

Behind Schmidt a big screen dropped down and came to life. Upon it appeared a large map with different locations marked around the Carinhall grounds. Mark said, "Have all these locations been checked?"

"Everyone had been over the grounds more than

once," Krause said. "They found tunnels, rooms, and hidden chambers, but no treasure which was said to have been left behind. We think that they came back and took it."

"By they, you mean SS-Oberst gruppenführer Gerhard Wolff?"

Krause glanced at Schmidt who smiled and nodded. The historian said, "Yes."

"My father thought it was still there, didn't he?" Mark asked.

"Yes," said Schmidt. "He talked about it a lot."

"If he thought it was still there, then it's still there."

"But it has been searched any number of times," Turow said. "We've looked carefully."

"Then you've not looked in the right place."

Turow gave Schmidt an exasperated look. The German billionaire said, "Just what we need, people; fresh eyes."

Mark said, "I read a part in the diary which mentioned an Angel's Treasure? Is that right?"

Turow nodded. "Yes."

"What does it mean?"

"It is a reference to an angel carved out of ivory and edged with gold leaf," Isabella said. "That's what has always been assumed, anyway."

"What if—"

"Here we go," Brooke said in a low voice.

Mark stared at her, still not sure how to take her. "What's that supposed to mean?"

"It was what your father always said," she replied. "What if?"

"You're not telling me anything new," Mark told her. "But *what if* it wasn't referring to the angel?"

"What else would it refer to?" Schmidt asked.

"Do we have a picture of the fountain at Carinhall?"

A few moments later a picture came up. But there was no longer any fountain present, just thick grass and debris. "Very funny," said Mark. "What about from when it was actually there?"

The picture changed.

"There," Mark said. "There is your angel."

Everyone in the room stared at the marble statue of the angel standing in the middle of the large fountain. "You're saying that the room is possibly under the fountain?" Schmidt asked.

Mark shook his head. "No, I'm saying it *is* under the fountain."

Turow said, "Surely it can't—"

"I guess there is only one way to find out," Schmidt said. "Have a look. Get it organized."

Everyone came to their feet and began filtering out of the room. "Mark, Brooke, stay behind please."

Mark and Brooke waited until the room was clear of everyone but them. Schmidt focused his stern gaze on Mark and said, "This being your first foray into the field could be dangerous, Mark, as we have recently found out. You do everything Brooke tells you to do, without question."

"I can take care of myself."

"She is in charge; therefore, you will do as she says."

"Fine."

"I trust that you will take all precautions, Brooke?" the German billionaire said.

"I'll not make the same mistake twice, sir."

"I know you won't, Brooke. Maybe you should take him downstairs and run him through a few things that might help him stay alive. See if he still *has it*."

"Sure."

———

"This is a Glock 19," Brooke said showing him the handgun. "It doesn't have a manual safety, but it does have other mechanisms in place to guard against accidental discharge. This one fires a nine-millimeter round from a seventeen round box magazine."

"I know what a Glock 19 is," Mark said. "Time in the military?"

Ignoring his sarcasm, Brooke took out a loaded magazine and went through the motions of loading it and putting a round into the chamber. Then she put on a pair of earmuffs before walking to the indoor firing range.

Mark had only enough time to put his in place before she started firing the weapon at a distant target.

Once the magazine was empty, she dropped it out and said, "Your turn."

She passed him the Glock and then a loaded magazine and said, "Now, load it without shooting yourself in the foot."

Her tone, whether intention or not, was patronizing. Mark couldn't be sure, but he wasn't impressed either way. For a start, she knew nothing about him, and her feelings were based on assumption.

Within a few moments Mark had the Glock loaded and firing at the target. When he stopped, he placed the weapon down on the table in front of him and said, "Satisfied?"

"Everyone hates a showoff," Brooke stated.

"Just like they do when being patronized," he shot back at her.

"Point taken. I'll get you one from the armory."

Mark shook his head. "Don't want one. Had enough of them when I served."

"You sure?"

"If the time comes when I really need a weapon, I'm sure I'll find one."

"Let's hit the gym, I want to see what you can do."

———

The Foundation gym took up most of one floor and included a heated pool for the staff to use. Before they started, Brooke looked at him and said, "You need some gym clothes. Go to the locker room and find some while I get changed."

"Something the right size?"

"Don't worry, we keep a stock of new clothes there in most sizes."

She was right and he found clothes to fit. He put on the shorts and a singlet top before returning to the open area where Brooke had laid out some tumbling mats.

"You ready?" she asked noticing the tattoos on his arms, now visible with his long sleeves gone.

He nodded. "Sure. I—"

The rest of his sentence was never voiced before Brooke started.

3

THE CARINHALL TREASURE

Carinhall Villa site

Mark moved and then stopped, reminding himself that he still hurt from the pounding that Brooke had given him the day before. But if he wanted to negotiate the broken ground between himself and where the fountain had been situated, he needed to do something. Brooke looked at him and asked, "Are you coming or what?"

Everything was overgrown with weeds, trees, vines, and long grass. Hidden amongst it all was what remained of the ruins. Abandoned towards the end of the war when the Russian Army was in sight, no less than eighty aircraft bombs were used to destroy it.

"The fountain was this way," Brooke told him. "Keep to the path."

"What path?" Mark asked.

"Just follow me."

They weren't alone. Isabella and Krause had accompanied them on this trip. The small group walked along the 'path' until Brooke stopped. "It's over there."

Mark moved in the direction that Brooke was indicating. After a dozen or so steps, he stopped. There was a large circular depression in the ground where the fountain had once stood. He looked around at the thick undergrowth thoughtfully.

"Well, where is it?" Krause asked pessimistically.

Mark ignored him and then walked towards a thicket to the north. Then suddenly he disappeared into the undergrowth. For a moment there was nothing, then he called to them, "Over here."

The three glanced curiously at each other and then strode forward, intrigued as to what Mark might have found. They pushed through the brush which formed kind of a natural barrier for what was behind it. A small clearing with what looked to be a half-buried concrete structure no bigger than six feet by six feet.

"Where has he gone?" Isabella asked.

Brooke frowned but then her expression changed to a darker one. "I'm going to kill him."

"What for?" asked Krause.

"For not fucking waiting."

A head popped up above the surface of the ground, framed by the concrete behind it. "Come on," Mark said, a large grin on his face.

"You were meant to wait for me," Brooke scolded him. "It's a good way to get into trouble."

They moved across to where Mark was and saw him standing in a hole. At its base was a tunnel which seemed to run back in the direction they had just come, towards the fountain. He waved at it with the pen light and said, "It's a bit tight but once you get through it opens out."

He ducked back down and squeezed through. Brooke looked at the other two. Isabella raised her hands, shaking her head and said, "I'm not going in there. I get claustrophobic in my bedroom."

"And I won't fit," said Krause rubbing his belly.

"Great," Brooke huffed. "I'll go."

"You're his security, that makes it your job," Krause pointed out with a shrug.

Brooke gave him a look before slipping into the hole then started to squeeze through.

Once she wriggled clear of the other side Brooke stood up and reached for her penlight. She flicked it on and flashed it around the inside walls. Most were covered with graffiti. Swastikas, words about Hitler being Germany's savior, and something about a Fourth Reich. To her front a light flashed, and Mark said, "I'm down here."

"Will you just slow the hell down?"

"This place is something, Brooke," he called back to her.

"What did I just tell you?"

He ignored her response and they continued along the tunnel. The smell of damp grew stronger as they approached the position where the fountain had been. In a couple of places, the concrete walls had a Parteiadler on them, but nothing really stood out. Another part of the tunnel had the concrete chipped away but there was nothing visible through the hole but black dirt.

When they reached the end of the underground corridor Mark stopped and sighed with open disappointment. Brooke stood beside him. "You didn't think it was going to be that easy, did you? If it were, the treasure would have been found by now."

He nodded then shone the light at the tunnel's abrupt end. "It's been caved in."

"Probably blown up with placed charges," Brooke said.

"I wonder what is beyond it?"

She shrugged. "By my calculations we're beneath the fountain."

"There has to be something," Mark said, his determination willing it to be so. Shining his light on the wall opposite, another Parteiadler stared back at him, its wings spread wide, in its claws, the swastika. Mark frowned. "You see that?" he asked Brooke as his light stayed fixed on the swastika.

She looked at it and said, "It's the wrong way around."

"Yes," Mark agreed. He moved back along the tunnel until he came to another; it was fine. He found the next one. It too was the right way around.

He turned back to Brooke. "You don't suppose that—"

"It would be too obvious, wouldn't it?" she replied with a shake of her head.

They hurried back along the tunnel until they reached the wall. Mark looked at it again, bent down and picked up a piece of concrete block and threw it at the wall. It bounced off, not leaving so much as a scar.

He shone his penlight around until it settled on a steel rod encrusted with patches of concrete, once used to reinforce the tunnel, obviously knocked loose when the tunnel was blasted.

Mark picked it up and hit the wall with it. The steel bounced off with enough force to fly past his ear. Had he not been controlling it, the object might well had hit his face. Changing his position slightly, he tried again for the same result.

"You might want to be careful with the way you're waving that thing around," Brooke cautioned him.

Ignoring her warning he hit the wall harder. This time the shockwave jarred up his arms to his shoulders making him gasp as the steel rod flew from his grasp.

"That's it!" Brooke growled. "There's nothing here. We're leaving."

"Wait," he told her and picked the steel up again.

Mark stared at the wall as he shone his light around it as though looking for a weakness. Then it stopped on the backward swastika. "I wonder."

"Brooke, shine your light there," he said.

She muttered something under her breath and then held the beam of her penlight on the swastika.

Mark stepped forward and swung the steel rod. He braced himself for it to fly back again, but the recoil never eventuated. Instead, the concrete gave way leaving a hole in the wall.

"Well, what do you know?" Mark said.

He bent a little and shone his light through the hole. "It's a room."

Using the steel rod, he chipped away at the wall until the hole was big enough to put his head and one arm through. He shone the light around for a while before withdrawing. Looking at Brooke who had her light shining upon him, he smiled and said, "We've found it."

———

It took two days to catalogue and remove everything from the underground bunker. The first was tied up with earth works which left the second for Isabella and Krause to photograph and log what they found. As it was brought out, Mark sat off to one side wondering what his father would make of the discovery.

"It is a wonderful find, you know?" the German billionaire said. "There are some great pieces in the collection, some thought to have been destroyed in Berlin when the Soviet troops invaded. But there was one piece amongst it which is more valuable than all the rest."

Mark looked at him waiting for the answer.

"We found Portrait of a Young Man by Raphael. It

alone is worth over one-hundred million dollars. It is an unbelievable find."

Schmidt waited for a reaction but there was none. He frowned and then said to Mark, "Your father?"

Mark nodded. "He would have been so excited about this place, this find."

"He would have, you're right. But he would also be happy that you were part of the team responsible for its discovery. Brooke told me it was you who found the room."

"It was just luck," Mark said dismissively.

"Luck had nothing to do with it. You are just like your father even if you don't see it."

Mark remained silent.

"We also found a few other items which have created a stir of excitement. But once we get back to Berlin, we can all go over them. You did well, young man. You should be proud. This is an amazing discovery."

"What will happen to it?" Mark asked.

"It will be transferred to Berlin and stored in a secure facility where it can be thoroughly examined and catalogued to be returned to its rightful owner, if there are any."

Mark nodded and said, "Here, have a look at this."

Schmidt put his hand out and took a tattered looking book from Mark. "What is it?"

"It looks to be some kind of ledger."

Mark was right, it was a ledger. And it was full of lost artifacts.

Somewhere in Germany

"They found the room at Carinhall, sir."

Behind the highly polished desk, a man looked up from his paperwork and stared at the person who had just spoken. "How did they do this?"

"I'm not sure."

"What are they doing?"

"They excavated the site so they could get the treasure out."

"How?" the man demanded. "How did they find it when we have looked for years and found nothing?"

"I'm not sure. They have a new team member with them. It was him who found it."

"Who is it?"

"Frank Butler's son."

"The one you killed at the lake?"

"Yes, sir."

"Then kill him too," the man said coldly.

"What about the items they found?"

"Take them. It all belongs to The New Nazi Party."

"Yes, sir."

———

Berlin, Germany

"Firstly, I would like to say great work to everyone involved with our discovery at Carinhall," Schmidt said aloud. His congratulations were met with claps and words of encouragement from those around him. "But what is even more exciting is that we found an item which may lead us to even more of what the Nazis stole during the war. Our Mister Butler has been looking through it ever since it was discovered. I haven't had a chance to ask him about it but I'm sure he has a lot to share."

Mark suddenly felt uncomfortable as every eye turned toward him. However, he gathered himself and climbed to his feet before walking to the front of the room to address those before him.

"While I was reading through the ledger," Mark began, "I asked Isabella for a list of what was found at Carinhall. Not one thing on her list matched with this."

A murmur rippled through the room. Mark went on, "Also, towards the back there were types of diary entries. I guess the Nazis liked to keep records of a lot of the things they did. However, it mentions three convoys which left Carinhall in January loaded with different treasures. There was even mention of Königsberg Castle."

That got their attention.

Königsberg Castle was reportedly the last known place the Amber Room had been kept before its disappearance.

The Amber Room had been a chamber decorated with amber panels backed with gold leaf and mirrors. Built during the 18th century in Prussia, it had adorned the Catherine Palace of Tsarskoye Selo near Saint Petersburg. That was before the Nazis got to it, dismantling it and ferrying it away, so the story goes, to Königsberg Castle.

Schmidt asked the question on everyone's lips. "Did it mention—"

Mark nodded. "Yes, there was a reference to something called 'The Room'. Also, there was mention of the *Wilhelm Gustloff*."

That brought them crashing back to earth.

The *Wilhelm Gustloff* had been sunk in the Baltic on the night of 30th January 1945 by the Soviet submarine S-13. Going down, it had taken 9,343 men, women and children. And, so it was rumored, one Amber room.

"The three convoys which left Carinhall in late January were loaded with stolen treasures each bound for a different destination. One lot was to go to Portugal, another to a port somewhere, the word was faded but I could make out part about a U-boat. One could assume that its destination was South America, and the third convoy's load was destined for a port on the Baltic."

"Danzig," growled Krause.

Mark nodded. "I'm afraid so."

"How do we know that what is in it is true?" Molly asked.

"I found a couple of signatures after a few entries," Mark explained. "I had Greg help me with identifying them. The first was easy because it was Göring's. The second belonged to a man named Gerhard Wolff. According to the information we discovered, Wolff was Göring's go-to man whenever it came to acquiring or moving treasure."

"We already know that," Krause stated.

Suddenly embarrassed, Mark stopped. Brooke could see his discomfort and said, "Don't listen to him. Just tell it like we don't already know. Keep going. And shut up, Werner."

Mark gave her a slight grin and Brooke returned it with a wink. He went on, "The fact is that the signature seems authentic which then lends authenticity to the ledger."

"Does it say where the destination for the shipment to Portugal actually was?" Isabella asked.

"No."

"That's fine," Krause said. "I'll get together with Molly, and we'll see if anything jumps out from any of the documents we have."

"That sounds good," Schmidt said. "Was there anything else, Mark?"

"The U-boat. Wolff had a number for it. U-2853."

He could see them all making notes, but it was Brooke who noticed the slight apprehension on Mark's face. "What is it, Mark? No secrets, we can't do our jobs otherwise."

He sighed and everyone stopped what they were doing to concentrate on him. "It's the ledger."

"What about it?" asked Schmidt.

"Where was it found?"

"It was sitting on a sixteenth century dresser," Isabella told him.

"Out in the open?"

"Yes."

"Does that seem odd to you?"

Isabella frowned. "Why?"

"Something that valuable left sitting on a table to be found by the next person who came along. It could have been the allies."

Brooke asked, "Are you thinking that it could've been left there as a decoy, intended to throw off whoever found it from the real destinations?"

Mark shrugged. "Maybe. Or perhaps I'm overanalyzing it."

"Overanalyzing things is what we do," Schmidt said as Mark sat down. "Never apologize for it. Alright, let's go and learn things. Dig deep because tomorrow the next adventure begins."

"What adventure is that?" Mark asked.

"Didn't I tell you? Tomorrow, you and Brooke are going to Portugal."

Mark glanced at her, and she gave him a sarcastic smile. "Great," he said. "It should be fun."

"One more thing," the German billionaire said. "I'm big on receipts. Keep them all."

Mark turned to Isabella. "He's joking, right?"

"Forget one and you will see," she replied giving him a white-toothed grin.

"Shit."

Ten minutes after the meeting broke up, Molly Roberts and Greg Turow sought Mark out. Each had a folder with documents for him to look through before he left with Brooke for Portugal. He took one look at the papers and blanched. "I'm expected to read all of these?"

Molly shrugged sympathetically. "With the good comes the bad, I'm afraid. But we can help you by filling you in on some of it. Kind of like a brief outline."

"So, make sure you damn well listen," Turow said.

Molly stared at him, her large brown eyes wide with expectation. Suddenly Mark burst with laughter. She placed her hands on her hips and asked, "What's so funny?"

"I'm sorry, it's the pink hair. You looked so serious for a moment but—"

"All right, very funny. I see I'm going to like you. Now, are you ready?"

Mark nodded.

"Portugal was a haven for stolen Nazi gold. The country supplied Germany with tungsten which it paid for with the gold stolen from other countries. Germany had started by paying in money, but someone started slipping counterfeit notes in, so the Portuguese demanded gold. The only way Germany could keep it up was to use all they could get from the countries they invaded."

"But Portugal was neutral." Mark said.

"It was but it dealt with both Great Britain and Germany," Molly told him.

Turow said, "After Switzerland, Portugal took in the second largest amount of stolen gold from the war. Something which the British let them keep after the fighting ceased. Some Portuguese man found documents at a railway station calculating some seventy-eight tons of Nazi gold passed through there. Almost one-hundred tons went through Swiss banks. Only some three and a half was returned after the war."

"So, what you're saying is that it is possible that some of the treasure from Carinhall did indeed go to Portugal," Mark theorized.

"I would say almost certainly," Molly said.

Turow continued. "There was no mention of where in Portugal that the treasure was sent, but we have a man in the country who could possibly point you and Brooke in the right direction."

Mark said, "I had a drill sergeant like her in the army."

"Can we continue?" Turow asked.

"Sure."

"OK. During the war there were two main banks taking the lion's share of the gold but by the time the war was over, and the Brits said they could keep it, most of it was gone and there was no record of where it went."

"What about art treasures and things like that?" Mark asked.

"We're not sure. We do know that towards the end of the war U-boats were reportedly in Lisbon."

"When?" Mark asked.

"Early February and again the month of the surrender."

"Which means they had the opportunity to load up with the treasure if the Nazis were going to do that," Mark said.

"Your powers of deduction are remarkable," Molly said, raising her eyebrows.

He matched her smile. "I've been told I'm handsome too."

"Oh, please. Now that we've connected all the dots the question is, or remains, what happened to the treasure?"

"What is the name of the man that we're to meet in Lisbon?" Mark asked.

"Carlton Greene," Turow said. "He's an ex-pat Brit. Historian who has been in Portugal for the past twenty years."

Mark looked at them both. "Thank you."

Turow patted him on the shoulder. "Now you have to do the hard part."

"Pardon?"

Molly pointed at the folders. "Start reading, sport."

4

THE TNNP

Lisbon, Portugal

Mark and Brooke flew into Lisbon the following day and caught a cab to their hotel. The Lisbon Palms Hotel with sparkling blue water pools, fitness centers, tropical style gardens, a cinema, theater. Everything expected of a five-star resort. Mark hadn't stayed in many nice hotels during his various travels, or never seen anything the like of this, and his countenance said as much.

"Close your mouth, you're drooling," Brooke said as they approached the reception desk.

"This place is frigging amazing," Mark said, ignoring her words.

The vast foyer floor was marble, the walls covered in a flocked wallpaper, the like of which he'd never seen before. Large artworks hung on the walls and looked to be expensive, and three large crystal chandeliers hung from a high ceiling covered in ornate plaster panels. Brooke's eyes took in everything surrounding them, apart from the décor, determined to keep them safe, while moving through the space.

They reached the long hardwood reception counter, its polished black marble top containing luminous flecks of mica. There were four uniformed clerks in attendance, three of whom were attending to other guests. A young woman of Sri Lankan descent smiled at them, revealing rows of even white teeth. "How may I help you?" she asked.

Brooke said, "We have a booking under the name Schmidt."

The young clerk smiled professionally at them once more and said, "I'll just check."

The clerk looked up. "I have your booking here. It's all paid for; all you need is a card to gain access to your room."

Brooke smiled. "Thank you."

"I won't be a moment."

She turned away and Mark said to Brooke, "You should do that more often."

"What are you talking about?"

"Smile. It changes your whole face, makes you quite attractive."

She glared at him. "And you should keep your opinions to yourself."

"There you go, doing it again," Mark sighed.

"Doing what?"

"Grouching again."

"I beg your pardon? I don't grouch. My job is to keep you alive, not make you feel all warm and damn fuzzy inside," Brooke protested.

"It seems that you grouch mostly at me."

"Just shut up."

The clerk came back and passed Brooke the key card. "There you are. Room three-oh-four. Third floor, off the elevator to your right. We'll have your baggage delivered to your room shortly. Enjoy your stay."

Turning away, they walked through several groups of people waiting to check in, past a multitude of lush indoor greenery, toward the double bank of elevators. Stepping into the first car to arrive, Brooke pressed the button for the third floor, and the doors closed smoothly; a slight jolt indicated the elevator's silent ascent had begun without so much as a hint of tinny muzak.

Only moments later, the alarm dinged, and the doors opened onto a wide, carpeted hallway. They came off the elevator and turned right. Mark said, "What's the rush?"

Brooke ignored him and kept walking, her footsteps brisk. She touched the card against the door lock and once it released, pushed the door open. "Get in there," Brooke snapped stepping aside.

She grabbed his arm and dragged him through the door, closing it behind her.

"Damn it, Brooke—"

"Be quiet," she whispered and began looking around the room. She started with the bathroom then the bedroom. When she emerged from there, she held a Glock in her hand.

Mark's eyes widened with realization that something was wrong. "What is it?"

"Down in the foyer I saw three men," she explained. "All of them had blond hair. One stood near the door as we entered. Another sat on a sofa in the middle of the foyer, reading a paper, the third was standing near the gift shop."

"So?" Mark said thinking that her imagination might have gotten the better of her.

"So, I saw two of them at the airport when we arrived."

Mark frowned. "Oh."

Brooke let out a frustrated sigh as she walked towards

the sliding glass door leading out onto the balcony that held several potted plants and patio furniture. She looked over the side and then came back in, closing the door behind her.

There was a knock at the door, and she froze. Mark watched her. "Who is it?" she called out.

"Room service," came the reply.

Brooke looked at him. "Get in the bathroom," she whispered.

Mark's reply was instant. "Why?"

She looked at him as though he were stupid.

He got the message. "Oh, we didn't order room service."

"I'll be there in a moment," Brooke called out.

Mark had only just started towards the bathroom when the door splintered as suppressed gunfire tore through it like a paper towel.

"Get down!" Brooke shouted and dropped to a knee.

Mark dived behind the bed as bullets whipped through the room.

What was left of the door was flung back and the three blond men she'd noticed earlier, forced their way into the room.

The Glock in Brooke's hand crashed, and the first man dropped to the floor, shot in the chest. The other two shooters let loose with their weapons, more automatic fire forcing Brooke to take cover from the deadly hailstorm.

She lunged towards the bed where Mark was hunkered down. Bullets followed her and he could feel the impact of each round as it punched into the mattress. "Don't suppose you have a spare one of them? I should have taken it when it was offered," he yelled.

"A bit late now. Just keep your ugly head down," Brooke ordered him. She fired off a couple more shots and dropped back down. She looked at him and said, "We need to get out of here."

"Just show me the way," he said with sarcasm. "Somehow I think the way we came in might be out of the question."

She gave him a sardonic smile. "Get ready to run."

"Where?" he demanded. "In case you haven't noticed the blond army kind of have the doorway blocked and are shooting at us."

"The balcony," she told him. "Just run and jump over the rail. Jump outward though or I'll have to tell Johann I lost another employee."

"What?"

Brooke fired off three more shots until the slide on the weapon locked back. She dropped down and reloaded. "You ready?"

"You're fucking crazy," he shot back at her. "Those guys are shooting at us."

A bullet snapped past her head, but Brooke's steely gaze never altered. "Just trust me."

"I don't have much choice, now do I?"

"Go now," she said and rose to fire off the rounds in her magazine, suppressing the attackers.

Mark ran. As fast as he could towards the...closed glass door. "Oh, no!"

He didn't see it but behind him, Brooke turned and fired her last couple of bullets at the glass. The window disintegrated under the shots and opened a clear path for Mark. His boots crunched on the glass as he passed through the opening, grinding beneath their soles. As he went, he leaped, placing one of his boots on the patio chair, using it as a springboard.

Then as he flew over the rail, he suddenly remembered the other reason he didn't want to jump. They were three floors off the ground.

___

When Brooke saw Mark clear the edge of the balcony, she tucked the Glock into her pants and immediately lunged to her feet and started running after him. Her only hope was that he'd jumped out far enough. As she flew over the rail, she looked down below and saw the white mess of water in the pool where he'd landed. Well, at least he wasn't a red splatter on the pavement.

The water was cold, and it took Brooke's breath away when she landed. Her feet touched the bottom and she pushed reflexively off the smooth tiles, her head breaking the surface of the water where she sucked in a big breath.

"Hey, you could have told me there was a pool down here," Mark said from the side.

"Just shut up and get out," Brooke growled stroking for the side, the numerous onlookers staring at them wide-eyed.

They clambered free of the pool, and both shook water from their hair before looking up at the balcony they'd just leapt from. The men who had blasted their way into the room suddenly appeared at the rail, looking down. One man saw the pair and pointed at them. The other sighted them and both lifted their weapons and opened fire.

"Run!" Brooke shouted as bullets hammered into the pavement around them. "Everyone, get out of here!"

She pushed Mark along in front of her, their wet clothes weighing them down, excess water spraying everywhere with each stride.

"Who are these guys?" Mark asked as they ran into the main building.

"I don't know."

"Excuse me! Excuse me!" The voice that carried across the foyer was directed at them. Mark looked and saw the young receptionist who had served them on arrival. "Is everything all right?"

"We're fine," Mark called back to her. "I wouldn't recommend jumping into the pool from our floor though. It's too cold."

She gave him a startled expression.

"Call the police!" Brooke snapped at her and gave Mark another shove toward the main entrance.

The young woman watched them go, a puzzled look on her face. It suddenly changed when the two shooters emerged from the elevator, waving their weapons around. One fired into the ceiling to clear a path for them. All the guests in the lavish foyer scattered, giving the gunmen a clear view of their quarry exiting through the doors out to the turnaround.

"*Da gehen sie!*" he called out and fired his weapon. *There they go!*

The glass of the main entrance doors shattered and fell like rain to the polished floor. Screams echoed around the foyer as the two remaining shooters ran toward the now doorless entrance and disappeared.

―――――――

"There, the taxi," Brooke called to Mark as the doors disintegrated behind them.

Mark changed direction and ran as fast as he could towards the cab. He reached it just before an elderly couple did and flung the door open. He looked at them before he climbed in and gave them a wan smile. "I'm terribly sorry, folks but we have a family emergency."

On the opposite side Brooke cast them an apologetic look before heaving open the door and getting in.

"Where to?" the driver asked in a heavily accented voice.

"Just drive," Brooke said. "Go now."

"I need a destination."

"I'll give you one when we get moving."

"My boss says that before we leave the—"

The back window shattered under a hail of gunfire spraying the interior with glass. Brooke instinctively pulled Mark down onto the rear seat and lay on top of him. "Fucking drive, damn it."

The driver let out a yelp and stomped on the gas. The vehicle's rear tires screeched as the cab shot forward and rocketed away.

Brooke sat up. "Are you alright?" she asked Mark.

"I'm fine," he replied. "Although having guys trying to kill you puts the senses on alert. That and jumping off a third-floor balcony. Haven't felt like that since Afghan."

"It was a little high," she agreed.

"You know what I'd like about now?" Mark said.

"What?"

"Some dry clothes."

She looked at him and then down at herself. Their clothes, sodden, clung to them like wet rags. She said to the driver, "We need to find a clothes store."

The man looked into the mirror. "Not a police station?"

"No, clothes store."

"But the men, they tried to kill you."

"Them? They were just saying hello."

The driver shrugged and said, "OK. I know a place."

"Thank you," Brooke said. "Now, you don't have a cell, do you?"

Berlin, Germany

"I need to know who these people are," Schmidt demanded of his people while he talked to only one. "Mister Webster, what have you found?"

"I was able to access the hotel security system and came up with images of these three men, one as you know is dead." Webster informed his boss. The large screen in front of them clearly showed three distinctive looking men. "I have a feeling, just by looking at them, that they are TNNP."

Schmidt sighed and said grimly, "I have more than a feeling you could be right."

To most people in Europe, the existence of the TNNP was just a rumor. But to Schmidt and his foundation, the TNNP were a reality. Now he was all but certain they were also responsible for the death of Mark Butler's father.

"Sir," Molly Roberts said interrupting Schmidt's thoughts, "we have another problem."

"It is certainly the day for it," he said. "Talk to me, Molly."

"The treasures discovered and recovered from the Carinhall site were stolen last night."

The German billionaire whirled; shock etched deep in his face. "What? How?"

"Armed men shot their way into the facility, murdered the guards, and took it all away."

"Do they have any idea who?" Schmidt asked.

"Not at this point," Molly told him.

The German billionaire turned to Webster. "Find me some footage. I want to see it for myself."

"Sir," Turow said to Schmidt. "Maybe we should call Brooke and Mark back."

"I already considered that as an option, but seeing as

they're already there, they might as well continue their task. Besides, Brooke is quite capable. I'm sure Mark is too. His military record was quite impressive."

"Until they're not."

Red hot eyes glared daggers at Webster. "Do you have something to say, Mister Webster? If you do, please share it with us all."

"No, sir. I have nothing to add yet."

"Then kindly keep your mouth sealed until it has something respectful to say. Now, since you seem to have a lot of time on your hands to criticize your comrades, I have another job for you."

"But—"

"But nothing. I want to know everything you can find out about the three men who tried to kill our people in Portugal. Understood?"

"Yes, sir."

"If you wish to act like a child, Mister Webster, you shall be treated as such."

"Sir."

"Let's hope they can find out something from Carlton Greene."

Lisbon, Portugal

Carlton Greene was a middle-aged man with dark hair quickly turning to gray. His face was lined, and his hands had a slight tremor as he looked through several documents which he hoped might hold some answers for the two people in front of him.

Both Brooke and Mark now wore dry clothes and were much more comfortable. Greene looked up at them. "The men who came after you, they all had blond hair?"

Brooke nodded. "Yes."

"Oh dear. It must be them."

"Must be who?" Mark asked.

Brooke gave Greene a warning glare, but it must have been misinterpreted for he said, "The New Nazi Party."

"Who?" asked Mark, not sure he'd heard the man right.

"The TNNP—"

"Are just a rumor that someone thought up about—"

"They are not," Greene said indignantly.

Brooke ground her teeth together. "Yes, they are."

"No. The New Nazi Party are real. They're behind a lot of trouble sweeping across Europe at the moment."

"What trouble?" Mark asked.

Brooke rolled her eyes and shrugged helplessly.

Greene continued. "Recently someone has been buying up a lot of artwork and artifacts related to the war, things that the Nazis stole. Those pieces that they couldn't buy they stole."

"Just stories," Brooke stated hoping to head the tale off.

"It's not." He passed Brooke a sheet of paper for her to read. "That list of artifacts was compiled not long after the war. Found hidden away in old mines, tunnels, cellars, bank vaults in Germany. You'll also notice that I have marks near individual items. Over the past few years these items were purchased by a company which doesn't exist."

"That doesn't mean—"

"Damn it, Brooke, will you stop!" Greene snapped. "You know they're out there and so does Schmidt. Even Frank knew."

She nodded. "Fine. When I saw them earlier today, I had a feeling that's who it was."

"You've had a run in with these guys before?" Mark asked.

"Yes," Brooke allowed. "These guys are possibly responsible for the death of your father. When I talked to Johann a while ago, he told me what they saw on the security footage."

Anger flared in Mark's eyes. "You never thought to frigging tell me this?"

"It was Johann's call. He wanted you focused on finding the treasure."

"But *you* still could have told me, Brooke," Mark growled. "How am I meant to trust you if it is only a one-way street?"

Brooke nodded. He had a point. "I'm sorry, Mark. From now on I'll be straight with you."

"Fine."

Brooke turned her attention to Greene. "You talked to Turow before we came here?"

The man nodded. "Yes. He said you were interested in a shipment of artifacts that the Germans made towards the end of January to Lisbon. Is that right?"

"Yes," Mark said, going on to tell him of the find at Carinhall and the mention of the room in the diary.

"By room, I assume that you're referring to the Amber Room?"

"We don't know," Mark said.

"Don't go down that rabbit hole, son. That thing is at the bottom of the ocean somewhere."

"What did you find out for us?" Brooke asked him.

"As you're aware, I've been looking into this for years now and have a lot of notes and scans and documentation about it all. Submarines came and went at the end of the war, taking passengers as well as other items. I believe that somewhere in the vicinity of twenty tons of gold were smuggled to South America in April alone."

"We have documents saying that there were U-boats here in early January," Mark told Greene. "It fits in with the timeline of what we're looking for."

"Let me look here," Greene said as he sifted through papers on his desk. His study was not large but was wall to wall books and papers in a somewhat organized chaos. "Here we are."

He held up a small notebook and started to thumb through it, muttering to himself as he went. Then, "Yes, February. According to this there were two U-boats in Lisbon early in the month. Both took on supplies and then left."

"What kind of supplies?" Mark asked.

"I don't know."

"Is there anyone who might?"

"Hmm. Almir might know," Greene said.

"Who is Almir?" Brooke asked.

"When he was a boy, he used to hang around the docks," Greene explained. "If anyone will know it will be him."

"Can we go and see him?" Mark asked.

"I think that should be okay."

5

THE BANK

Lisbon, Portugal

The elderly man, Almir, appeared to have one foot in the grave and wasn't far from having the other one join it. The lines on his face resembled canyons from some far-off planet; he was hard of hearing; his voice was cut from gravel, and his glasses were so thick they might have been mistaken for the bottom of a glass cola bottle. But his mind was sharp which was what was important to them.

"Almir," Greene said in the man's native tongue. "This is Brooke and Mark."

"What?"

"Brooke and Mark."

The man in his eighties eyed them suspiciously. "What do they want?"

"They want to talk to you," Greene replied.

"Does he speak Spanish?" Mark asked.

"I don't know," Greene said.

"Do you speak Spanish?" Mark asked.

The old man nodded. "What do you want?"

"To ask you some questions about the U-boats that were here in Lisbon."

"What?"

"The U-boats in Lisbon," Mark said louder.

The old man looked at Greene, a confused expression on his face. Brooke muttered something under her breath which Mark couldn't make out. Then he had an idea. "Give me your cell," he said to her.

During the shopping sojourn for dry clothes, they had also replaced their cell phones, the sim cards the only thing salvageable from the old ones.

"Why?" Brooke asked.

"I'll show you," Mark said taking his own out. He also took out the earbuds and plugged them in. Then when Brooke gave him her cell, he dialed his number, answered, and then gave it to the old man. Almir gave him a confused look.

Mark leaned forward and took the earbud and put it in the old man's ear. Next Mark put Brooke's cell up to his mouth and said in Spanish, "Can you hear me better now?"

Almir's face lit up with a broad grin. He nodded and said, "Is good. I hear you good."

"Great. We want to ask you about the U-boats that came to Lisbon towards the end of the war."

The old man nodded. "Yes, U-boats come. I see them when at the docks."

"Were there many?" Mark asked.

Almir shrugged. "Nine, ten."

"That many?" Mark reacted, raising his eyebrows.

"Yes. Most came in the darkness."

"What did they do?"

"Towards the end they took men, women, families."

"Where to?"

Almir shrugged. "I do not know."

"South America?"

The old man shrugged. "It is possible I suppose. They all seem to say that."

"Did you see any of the U-boats being loaded?" Mark asked.

"Which ones?"

"The ones in early February?"

"Yes."

Mark felt his nerves start to jangle. "Do you know what they were putting on them?"

"Mainly supplies."

"That's it?"

"Yes."

"No large crates, boxes, things like that?"

Almir shook his head. "No. Only the ones in April had those."

Mark felt his heart sink. He nodded and said, "Thank you for your time."

The old man put up his hand. "Wait. There is one place you might try."

Mark waited for him to continue. "Try the *Banco de Portugal*. They were one of the biggest ones that stored Nazi gold. They might have something."

"I know the manager," Greene said. "He should help us."

Maybe it wasn't a complete waste after all. "Thank you, Almir."

————

The building was old, built in the eighteen hundreds, maybe earlier. The interior had been extensively refurbished, and the floor was polished granite. There were tellers at counters and seven or eight desks out in the open where neatly attired men and women sat talking to clients. There were security cameras in each corner of the room as well as along the walls. Finally, there were four guards armed with compact Heckler and Koch MP5s.

"Bet you're glad you never brought your Glock with you. Do they have enough security in this place?" Mark asked Brooke as he looked around.

"They never used to," Greene said. "The *Banco de Portugal* has been robbed twice in the past seven years. The first time the thieves cleaned out the vault. Came up through the floor like in some eighties action film. The time following that they just went after the ready cash."

Mark snorted. "Bet they never got much."

"Six-million."

The amount staggered him. "You're kidding?"

"It's true," Greene told him.

"Shoot."

They approached the counter attended by a female clerk. She wore a red dress and bright red lipstick. "How can I help?"

Greene said, "We would like to see Mister Nunes."

"Do you have an appointment?"

"No, we don't. But if you could tell him that Carlton Greene is here it might go a way to helping out."

She gave him an even-toothed smile. "One moment please, I'll see what I can do."

They moved to one side to wait out of the way. Mark looked around the room, taking in all the intricate work-ings on the walls and the art which hung on them. Then his eyes stopped as he focused on one in particular. "Good grief."

Brooke looked at him. "What's wrong?"

"The painting on the wall."

They all looked at the artwork. "What about it?"

"It's Portrait of a Young Man by Hans Memling," he hissed.

"Are you sure?" Greene asked.

"Absolutely, I'm sure. Come with me."

They followed him over to the wall and stood in front of the picture. Portrait of a Young Man by Hans Memling had been painted in the 15th Century. When taken by the Nazis, it had been hanging in the Uffizi Gallery in Florence, Italy in August 1944. It had been appropriated along with many others and put into a truck. The truck had headed north, never to be seen again, along with the artwork.

Greene said, "It doesn't look like it."

Mark took out his cell and brought up a picture of the artwork in question. "Look at this and compare the two. There have been a couple of rings added to the other fingers, the flowers added to the mantel, which is also added, and the crucifix."

"That would mean that they painted over it," Brooke said. "Who would do that with such a valuable painting and then hang it in public view?"

"What better place to hang it," Mark countered as he took a picture. "Plus, I recall reading something about how the Nazis were experimenting with a paint that could be used and then removed without leaving any trace."

"I remember something about that too," Greene said. "But this—no it can't be."

"I guess we'll find out. I just sent a picture to Isabella."

"Carlton, it is good to see you," a voice from behind them said.

They all turned and looked at the rotund man standing before them. Greene smiled. "Cipriano, my friend, likewise."

"It is a good painting, is it not. It was painted at the turn of the century by a local artist."

"Very nice," Greene said. "Mark here saw it and thought he'd like to take a closer look while we waited."

"Ahh, a man with great taste, no?" Nunes commented turning his gaze to Mark. "You are the gentleman in question?"

Mark nodded. "Yes."

He held out his hand and Nunes took it. "I'm Cipriano Nunes."

"Mark Butler. This is Brooke—ah—" He looked at her for help.

"Brooke Reynolds," she said leaning forward taking the big man's hand.

He took it then let it go. "What do I owe the pleasure?" Nunes asked.

"Can we talk somewhere a little more privately?" Greene asked.

"Certainly. My office should suffice."

Showing them into an office furnished with a large antique desk, a sofa, and handcrafted chairs, they took in a large cabinet filled with numerous different kinds of artifacts. As Mark looked around, he noticed many paintings on the walls, then crossed to the cabinet and ran his gaze over the treasures within. Then he took a seat on the couch beside Brooke while Greene took a chair along with Nunes. The bank man sighed. "Now, shall we discuss why you are here?"

Mark's cell buzzed on silent in his pocket. He dug it out and looked at it, earning him a jab in the ribs from Brooke's elbow.

Greene said, "We would like to know if we could look through some old records, Cipriano, please?"

The man frowned. "Why, might I ask?"

"We have reason to believe that a German convoy came to Lisbon in late January, early February of nineteen forty-five, carrying artifacts, and possibly gold. Knowing the history of this establishment, if it were carrying gold then something should be notated in the archives."

The man shook his head sorrowfully. "I'm afraid that is impossible."

"But why?" Greene asked. "You have let me look before when I wanted to do research."

"Change of policy," Nunes said.

"Change of policy or something to hide?" Mark asked pointedly.

Brooke placed her hand on his thigh and gave it a warning squeeze.

"I beg your pardon?" Nunes said acting indignant.

"Mark," Brooke warned him from out of the side of her mouth.

Mark leaned forward, staring hard at him. "I'm sorry, Mister Nunes, I spoke out of turn."

"That is fine, apology accepted."

"But I can't get over that painting that we saw when we came in."

"I'm not sure what you mean."

"Shit," Brooke muttered.

"How long has it been here?" Mark asked.

"I'm not sure."

"I think I know. I would guess around nineteen forty-five. Delivered by a Nazi truck into the bank's hands for safe keeping. It's not some painting from the turn of the century like you said. It's Portrait of a Young Man by Hans Memling."

The name landed like a brick in the middle of the room and Mark saw the man wince. "I—I'm not sure what you are saying?"

"Really," Mark said, coming to his feet. "My father was right into antiquities and artifacts. Stuff like that. He was never home but whenever he was there was always a notebook, textbook, or magazine laying around. I was very curious when I was a young boy, and I learned a lot. Then I studied it some myself. For instance, let's have a look at your cabinet."

He stopped in front of it and pointed at a little statue. "Incan if I'm right but I'm betting it's fake. The blood diamonds in its eyes aren't though. The small vase. From China, Ming, eighteenth century. I bet you got that from a Japanese collector who liberated it in the Second World War. That little statue near the end. Made of marble, Rome, perhaps Second Century."

Nunes had paled somewhat, and Brooke watched Mark's performance with amazement. The young man walked over to a painting on the wall. He looked at it for a moment before taking it down.

"You cannot touch that," Nunes blurted out.

Without hesitation Mark smashed the frame on the corner of the bank man's expensive desk. The frame shattered and Mark separated the two artworks which were inside it. "Well, well. The first one isn't much but the second is a work by French artist Allard. If I remember rightly titled Man with Dog. Weird name for a painting but it is what it is. Shall I go on, Mister Nunes?"

The bank man looked apoplectic and Brooke feared that he was close to a heart attack. His brow was laden with sweat, his face ashen. He reached inside his coat pocket for a handkerchief and mopped at his face.

"All we wanted was to check for an entry in an archive, Mister Nunes," Mark said in a soft voice. "But now the Schmidt Foundation is involved and I'm pretty sure they're on their way here. Possibly Interpol as well."

Brooke glanced at him. He said, "The message was from Isabella. She's certain about the painting."

"I see."

Greene said, "I'm sure it would be in your best interest, and the bank's if you helped us out, Cipriano. Even if it is a dead end."

Nunes nodded. "Come with me, I will take you downstairs."

They followed him out the door. Mark and Brooke trailing. She said, "You are just a bundle of information."

"Living with my father I couldn't help but be interested," he replied.

Then Brooke's voice hardened. "Just be thankful it paid off."

"I always am."

Nunes led them downstairs to a vault fitted with multiple rows of shelving from floor to ceiling. He found the one he wanted and moved about halfway along before stopping in front of a box. He passed it to Mark and said with more than a hard edge to his voice, "Good luck. Don't drop it on your foot. It would be a shame."

Brooke said, "I'd get ready for Interpol if I were you."

Going through the files, they sifted through jumbled bundles of papers with statistics and documentation covering the whole of the 1945 year, making it difficult to find what they required. But an hour later, Greene held up a sheet of paper and said, "I think I might have something here."

Mark and Brooke moved to look over his shoulders.

"What does it say?" Brooke asked.

"It indicates that at the end of January trucks delivered a shipment of gold to the bank."

"We're not after gold. The diary indicates artifacts, paintings, even sculptures," Mark told him.

"Wait," Greene said. "It also says there were three other crates, but it doesn't say what was in them."

"Does it say what happened to them?" Brooke asked.

"No, but there are numbers for each of them."

Mark scanned the vault slowly, contemplating the job

ahead and what else it would take to get the job done. "We're going to need more people."

———

It took two days of looking before they found even a hint of what they sought. Tracking the gold shipments was the easy part. In September of 1945, not long after the end of the war, it had been removed from the bank by the Portuguese government. But by the time they got through 1945 the three searchers still hadn't found the corresponding numbers they were looking for.

This made it necessary to move into 1946. And since Nunes was busy with Interpol officers, it fell to a young female bank clerk to find for them what they required. Then came 1947, 1948, 1949. On the second day the same young clerk who was helping them said, "You know all these files were put onto computer a few years back? It took the best part of a year to do it."

For a moment Mark thought Brooke might try to strangle the fresh-faced young woman, so he stepped in front of her and said, "It would have been nice to know this earlier."

She shrugged.

"Would you be able to find these numbers for me?" Mark asked with a pleasant smile.

"Yes. I'll be back in a moment."

She hurried away, her high heels clunking loudly on the hard floor. Mark turned to look at Brooke who said, "I could happily choke the living—"

"Be nice, Brooke," Mark said cutting her off.

"I'll show her fucking nice," she hissed.

It took around fifteen minutes for the young clerk to return. She passed over three printed sheets of paper and said, "There you are."

Mark looked at the numbers first. Every single one matched up. Then he looked at the contents and his eyes widened. "Holy shit."

"What do we have?" Greene asked.

"Caesar's Bust, Madonna With Child, The Stone Breakers which apparently wasn't lost in the Dresden Firestorm, the same with a couple of Ernst Ludwig Kirchner's works that the Nazis were meant to have destroyed. We also have tapestries—good grief the list just goes on and on. Some of this stuff was not listed in the ledger."

He passed it over to Greene who read through it, shaking his head before finally passing the sheet over to Brooke. Meanwhile, Mark read through the other two. "This is unbelievable."

"The question is," Brooke said, "where did it all go?"

"According to this they were moved in nineteen fifty-one," Mark replied. "They were signed for by..." he frowned.

"By whom?" Greene asked.

"Heinrich Wolfsjunge."

"How strange," Greene said.

"What's strange?" Brooke asked.

"Wolfsjunge is like wolf cub in English."

Greene frowned. "Wolfsjunge, Wolfsjunge, Wolfsjunge. Why should that be familiar?"

"Gerhard Wolff," Mark told him. "The man who did a lot of acquisitions for the Reich."

"That's him," Greene said with a snap of his fingers. "Could that be him?"

"I don't know. We need to get the information to the Foundation to see what they make of it."

6

THE BOOKKEEPER

Berlin, Germany

"Where are we with Heinrich Wolfsjunge?" Schmidt asked his team.

"Still looking," Molly told her boss.

Turow looked up and said, "We thought we could trace it back to Gerhard Wolff but there isn't any relative, especially a son with the name Heinrich."

"Well, there must be something," the German billionaire replied. "What about the treasures from the lists?"

"That is huge," Isabella said to him. "Some of the items were thought to have been destroyed. If we can locate them, it would totally rewrite history."

"If we can find them," Schmidt said. "Has there been any progress with the other shipments that were talked about in the diary?"

"Nothing other than the U-boat number that we already know about."

"I might have something," Webster said from behind his computer console.

"Please enlighten us, Mister Webster," Schmidt said.

"The artifacts were never there," he told them. "Everything on that list was never in that bank."

Everyone stopped what they were doing and stared expectantly at the young man.

Turow's gaze hardened. "If this is one of your games, Webster, I'm going to come over there—"

"Take it easy, Gregory," he chided the man. "You look like you're about to pop."

"Mister Webster—" Schmidt began.

"I've searched through everything we have, the CIA has, or had. Old OSS and SOE files, along with the MFAA looking specifically for things on that list. I came up with nothing. Then I found two sentences in a document which says everything. I'll put it on the screen."

A few moments later the two sentences appeared.

Checked Banco de Portugal and discovered all gold deposits which were left for the government. Nothing else was found.

"Where did you find that?" Schmidt asked.

"In a document addressed to none other than Winston Churchill from someone named Walter Hammond."

"Hammond was part of the Monuments, Fine Arts, and Archives section which was set up towards the end of the war to find lost treasures," the German billionaire said.

"Which means that he went through the bank with a fine-tooth comb," Molly told them. "If there was something there, he would have found it."

"What about what Mark and Brooke found at the bank?" Krause asked.

"Most likely acquired afterward."

"The others need to talk to Nunes again."

"We seem to be forgetting the paperwork they found," Krause pointed out.

"Papers can be forged," Molly reminded him.

"It seems to be a lot of trouble to go to."

"Well worth the effort if it covers what really happened to them," Molly said.

"In other words," Schmidt said, "we've run into a brick wall."

Turow said, "We know they left Carinhall for three different destinations. Or that was the plan. We still have two leads to follow-up on. We must be onto something because why else would TNNP be trying to stop us?"

"All right," Schmidt said. "After Brooke and Mark talk to Nunes again, we look at the other two options. Which one do we pick?"

"Send them to South America," Isabella said. "I've always wanted to go back."

Schmidt was surprised. "You want to go with them?"

"It will be good to be on hand if they find something."

"It could be dangerous."

"I can take care of myself."

"All right. Once they get back from Portugal, I'll organize the flights. In the meantime, see if you can find anything that links our U-boat to South America."

—————

Lisbon, Portugal

"Schmidt wants us to talk to Nunes again," Brooke said to Mark and Greene. "They hit a bit of a snag."

"What kind of a snag?" Mark asked.

"It seems that the intel we just gained is fake." She went on to tell them the whole story.

"What if it isn't?" Mark said.

"Mark—"

"Wait, Brooke, just hear me out. What if it was real only it never made it this far?"

"Gee, Mark, you're starting to do my head in. Let's head over to the Interpol offices and see if they'll let us talk to Nunes. I'll dial ahead."

After a few minutes on her cell, Brooke said, "He's been released. He's at his house."

"I know where he lives," Greene said. "Let's go."

———

Nunes lived on the outskirts of Lisbon on a five-acre estate. The building was three floors and made of block plastered with white render. The gardens were well established, and the gravel drive went all the way up to form a turnaround at the front steps. However, to get there, they had to negotiate two large wrought iron gates blocking the entrance.

Greene leaned out the driver's window of his Range Rover and pressed the button on the intercom. He waited but nothing happened. He tried again with the same result.

"Maybe he's not here," Brooke said.

"Or he's not answering," Greene said.

"Did you see that?" Mark asked.

"See what?"

"I saw movement at the window on the second floor."

"I didn't see anything," Brooke stated.

The rear door opened, and Mark climbed out. "Where are you going?" Brooke hissed.

"To talk to Nunes."

Before she could protest further, Mark had scaled the fence like a monkey and disappeared over the other side. "Great," she growled. "Just great."

She started to climb out of the vehicle then turned to Greene and said, "Don't go anywhere."

Brooke vaulted the fence with ease, a testament of her daily workout regimen. She then jogged after Mark, grabbing him by the sleeve when she caught up with him. "Slow your roll, Captain America," she said in a low voice. "We don't know what we're walking into."

"What do you propose?" he asked.

She took the Glock from her waistband. "Keep your head down and follow me."

They kept to the foliage of the expansive garden, using it to screen their approach to the house. They circled around to come up to the back of the house through the swimming pool area with its sandstone pavers and tall palms.

There was a set of French doors that led from the pool area which beckoned the two intruders towards them. But instead of going straight at them, Brooke stayed clear of the line of sight from them just in case someone was in there looking out.

She pressed her back against the hard, white stucco wall and made sure Mark stayed behind her. Looking at him, she gave a stern, no-nonsense stare. "Stay behind me and do whatever it is I tell you to do, got it?"

He nodded and Brooke said, "We don't have to do this."

"We need to talk to him," Mark said.

"Okay. Let's go."

Brooke peered around the corner of the stucco wall and in through the glass of the French doors. It looked to be a large living room and from what she could see it was clear. She reached out and touched the doorhandle. It moved easily so she was able to open the door.

Mark followed her inside. The room was full of

antiques of all shapes and sizes. Even the artworks on the walls. Nunes was definitely a collector.

"Stay close," Brooke said to him in a soft voice.

With Mark behind her she crept across the room, stopping when she reached a large, dark wooden door that was closed. Turning the handle until it snicked open, Brooke put her eye up to the crack and peered through. Beyond the door was a large foyer with a staircase to the left which appeared to hug the wall up to the next floor.

"What do you see?" Mark asked.

Brooke's head snapped around. "Be quiet. You want whoever is here to know that we're inside as well?"

"Sorry, I was—"

"Can it." This time the stare was withering. Mark nodded and pressed his lips together.

Brooke opened the door wide enough for them both to slip through it. The foyer had a beautiful slate floor and more art works on the wall. One in particular caught Mark's eye. He tugged at Brooke's shirt and opened his mouth to speak. But before he could her hand shot out and clamped over it. She leaned in close and whispered into his ear, "If you get us sprung it won't be the bad guys who shoot you, understood?"

He nodded.

Voices suddenly emanated from somewhere on the second floor and sounded as though they were getting closer. Brooke froze briefly then glanced around the foyer. The next thing Mark knew he was being propelled towards a closed door by a hand pressed firmly into the middle of his back.

Fortunate for them, the door was unlocked, and he was able to get it opened. The pair pushed through, and Brooke closed it, so it was not quite shut. She kept an eye to the crack and watched as two armed men came down the stairs. They were conversing in German. One carried a book.

All at once Mark began tapping her on the shoulder. She shrugged it off, but he didn't stop. His incessant tapping continued, if anything, became more urgent. Brooke turned and glared at him. "What?"

He pointed across the room of what appeared to be a study to the person sitting in a hand-carved chair and whispered, "It's him."

Brooke's eyes narrowed as her gaze focused on the man in the chair. It was him. Nunes. Although it was hard to tell because of the hole in his forehead and blood on his face. "Oh, no."

Brooke shut the door and locked it. "See what you can find in that desk. And hurry it up while I try to get us out of here."

Mark hurried across to the desk and started going through the drawers. He grabbed a couple of what looked to be diaries. He was about to open a second drawer when the door handle rattled. He stopped and looked across at Brooke who was examining a window. She glanced at him and said, "Keep going."

The third drawer slid open, and he riffled through it. Mark was about to close it when he found a thumb drive. He stuffed it into his pocket.

"Can we go now?" he asked.

Before Brooke could answer, the door imploded as the men on the other side began firing their weapons into it. Mark dropped to the floor as bullets buzzed across the room. He looked over at Brooke and shouted, "This is your fault. If I'd wanted people shooting at me all the time, I'd have stayed in the military. I'm not anymore, but still, that's all I'm getting."

"How is it my fault?" she shot back at him. "You were the one who jumped the fence."

Angry, Brooke picked up a second chair and threw it at the window. The glass shattered and it tumbled out through the new opening. "Get out the window," she ordered and started using her Glock, firing at the door.

Mark didn't need to be told twice and ran to climb through the window. He hissed as a piece of glass sliced into his left hand, but kept going. As soon as he was out, Brooke followed him. She landed cat-footed beside him and said, "Move."

"Next time can we use the front door?"

"Shut up and keep going."

They ran around the house and along the drive towards the front gate. Behind them the front door burst open, and the intruders appeared, opening fire with their weapons and filling the air with the snap of bullets.

The pair scrambled over the front gate and jumped into Greene's car. "Get moving!" Brooke yelled as the men appeared.

Greene stomped on the gas and the car shot backward at an alarming rate. He hit the brakes and then hurriedly wrenched the shift into drive. The wheels spun as he hit the gas once more. "What did you do?" he called back over his shoulder.

"We didn't do anything," Brooke told him. "But those guys killed Nunes."

"What happened?" Wolfsjunge asked.

"They broke in and gained access to the study."

"What did they take?"

"I don't know."

"Well then, what did you find?"

"Nothing."

"Could they have found anything that might compromise everything that has been worked towards over the past seventy-five years?"

"I don't know."

"You don't know?"

"No, sir."

"We have accumulated a lot since the end of the war but there are still many of the Reich's treasures out there. We can't let them discover them before we do. My source within the foundation says that they are going to South America in search of the U-boat next. You will go there too."

"Why?"

"Because if they find it, they could possibly put the next piece of their little puzzle together."

"But we could find them here and finish it before they leave."

"No," Wolfsjunge said. "There has been too much killing in Europe. Watch them in Argentina and then make them disappear. Did you burn the house?"

"Yes, sir."

"Good." There was a long pause, and then, "Tell me this, how did some of the finest works happen to be in the bank and not in our possession?"

"He said he liked them."

"But he told us they were fakes."

"Yes, sir. That's what he said."

"Now they are beyond our reach. Very disappointing."

"Yes, sir."

"At least we have the Carinhall treasure in our grasp. That is something, I suppose."

"Yes, sir."

"That will be all."

"Yes, sir."

The line went dead.

Mark flinched as Brooke dabbed antiseptic onto the cut across his palm. He uttered a low growl deep in his throat and she said, "Why are men such sooks?"

"Easy enough for you to say; you're not the one bleeding."

Brooke ceased what she was doing and lifted her singlet top to expose a thick scar on her left side. "North Africa. I survived. Now, stop complaining about a little scratch on your hand and let me finish."

Greene appeared. He'd been looking through the diaries Mark had taken from the desk before going out the window. Brooke looked at him and asked, "Did you find anything?"

He shook his head. "Most of it was artworks and artifacts he'd acquired along the way. He did make mention of the ones we found at the bank, and it seems he picked them up from different auctions throughout Europe."

"Can we use it?" Mark asked.

Greene shook his head. "No. They're underground auctions. Black market. They spring up and then disappear. Interpol have tried to get inside them, but they keep coming up empty."

"What about the thumb drive?" Mark asked.

"That was something different altogether. As far as I can tell it is a complete list of artworks and artifacts that came into the Nazis' possession over the course of the war. I'm not sure what the significance of it is but it has to be worth something."

Brooke finished dressing Mark's hand and said, "There you go, cream pie, as good as new."

"Thanks, Brooke."

She gave him a wry smile and got up from where she was seated. Mark, however, remained where he was, thoughts running through his head. Greene frowned at him and asked, "What are you thinking about?"

"You said that the diaries were mostly about artworks and artifacts that Nunes had bought over the past years; is that right?"

"That's right."

"And there was some mention of the things we found in the bank?"

Greene nodded. "Right again, only there were a couple of notes saying that they were fake. Portrait of a Young Man by Hans Memling included."

"But that wasn't a fake," Mark said.

"How do you know?" Brooke asked.

"When you have a father like mine you learn things. I would stake my life on it that the painting was the real thing."

"Then why would he say it was fake?" Greene asked.

"So, he could keep it, I guess, so he says it's fake," Mark replied. "I bet in fact that everything marked as a fake in the diaries is actually the real thing."

Greene asked another question, "Why would they kill him?"

"To silence him," Brooke said.

"Really?"

"The thumb drive," Mark said. "You said as far as you could tell it was a list of what the Nazis stole during the war?"

"Yes."

"Can you show us?"

"Follow me."

They went into Greene's study where he brought the list up on a screen. It appeared to be exactly what he'd described it as: a list of stolen Nazi treasure. Except some items were noted in different colors. The bulk of items listed were written in black, some were in red, more in blue, and then a few in green. "That's curious," Mark said.

"What is?" Brooke asked.

"They're notated in different colors."

"The question is, why?" Greene said.

Mark stared at the list, lost in contemplation for a long time before giving his theory. "Look at the green ones. This one here, Picking Peas by Camille Pissarro. If I remember rightly it was stolen in 1943 from some guy named Bauer. He was sent to an internment camp. A few years ago, it turned up in an American collection and the new owners were forced to return it. All these green ones that I can remember were given back to their rightful owners when found. The red ones are easier. They are all reported destroyed in the war."

"What about the black and blue ones, genius?" Brooke asked.

Mark studied the list once more. He nodded and said, "The black ones are still missing."

"And the blue?"

A few more moments and then, "It leaves just one reason. They're the ones they've already recovered."

"Who?"

"TNNP. Nunes was their bookkeeper."

"Now you're clutching at straws," Brooke said to him.

"It's not that unbelievable," Mark told her. "Nunes was in a great position to do what they needed. I'll bet that they killed him to keep him quiet."

"But he kept his files on the thumb drive," Greene said. "That's what they were after."

"We need to get it back to Johann," Brooke said. "They might be able to get something useful off it."

7

THE U-BOAT

Berlin, Germany

"I think you're right," Turow stated as they all gathered around the table at the Schmidt Foundation. "I concur with your theory that he was indeed their bookkeeper."

"Did you find much?" Mark asked hopefully.

Turow shook his head. "Webster went through it and could find nothing hidden away inside. All we have are the lists."

"What about the diaries I took from the drawer?"

"Nothing much at all."

"A waste of time then," Mark said.

"No," said Isabella hurriedly. "Those lists on the thumb drive were very comprehensive. On a positive note, at least we know that some of the artifacts we thought long gone are still intact. Even if we don't know where they are."

"Don't be so hard on yourself," Schmidt said. "We have been able to get our hands on some real gems since you joined our team."

"Only to lose them again," Mark pointed out.

Schmidt's expression turned grim. "We're well aware of that."

There was a drawn-out silence before the German billionaire said, "Let's have a look at the U-boat theory. Isabella wants to go to South America with you."

Mark looked her and nodded when he saw that she was excited. "I say OK."

She smiled broadly at him, and he returned one of his own.

"Great," Brooke groaned. "I have to babysit two of them."

"I don't need babysitting," Isabella and Mark retorted simultaneously. The pair laughed, looking at each other.

"We'll see."

"What do we know, Werner?" Schmidt asked Krause.

"From the research I've completed over the past few years I discovered that there were possibly three confirmed U-boat sightings in Argentina. Two were Type Fourteen and the last one was a Type Twenty-One. All three were seen in Buenos Aires. The first two were said to have been there around October, November of 1944. The last one was reported there in March."

"What was a Type Twenty-One?" Mark asked curiously.

"They were built towards the end of the war. Not many of them saw combat. The thing about these U-boats was that they were designed to remain underwater for great periods of time and travel over long distances."

"And there were only three sightings in Argentina?"

"Three confirmed sightings. There were others but they were filed in the fantasy box."

"What happened to the three that were confirmed?"

"No one knows. Rumor has it that at least one of them went up the Parana River. But that is just rumor."

"Where would they go if they went up there?"

"This is where it gets interesting," Krause said. "Take a look at the screen."

All heads turned to look at the large monitor. It came on and a map appeared. "What are we looking at?" Turow asked.

"La Cumbrecita. It was built by a German family back in the nineteen-thirties." The screen changed and pictures of Bavarian cottages, alpine chalets. "Over time they had their own little village. The man's name was Helmut Cabjolsky. I'm not sure what his wife's name was but the story goes that she was half Jewish so they couldn't return to Germany. It did cause some problems in Argentina as well."

"They built this place?" Mark asked.

"Yes."

"Do you think that the treasure was taken to be stored there?"

"No. There is another valley close by where another compound was said to have housed some high-ranking German Nazi Party members who escaped at the end of the war. They called it Neue Hoffnung. Or New Hope. If there was to be any likely hiding place, then that would be it."

"Why didn't they just live in La Cumbrecita?" Molly asked.

"Because of Helmut Cabjolsky's wife," Schmidt said. "It would be like living beside the people they swore to eliminate."

"All right," Mark said. "Let's say it's true that the U-boat reached South America and went up the river. Surely the place has been picked over before now."

"Says he who found the treasure at Carinhall," Brooke said with a little sarcasm.

Schmidt said, "You will meet a guide in San Isidro. He will take you anywhere you need to go. He is also a historian with a specialty for the German/Argentine period."

"Do we go to New Hope first?" Mark asked. Then he chuckled. "Sounds like the first Star Wars movie."

Schmidt said, "The plane leaves at ten tomorrow morning."

————————

San Isidro, Argentina

Their contact's name was Benicio Garcia. He was a thin man with dark hair and blue eyes. Mark figured him to be somewhere in his late thirties. They met him in a small office where he ran an artifacts business.

"It is a pleasure to meet you," he said to them with a broad smile. "My name is Benicio."

Brooke introduced them all. "I'm Brooke, the lady eyeing your collection is Isabella, and this guy is Mark."

"Hi."

"Ciao."

"That there is an—"

"Incan statue from the fourteen hundreds," Isabella finished. "It is bellissima."

He smiled. "Yes, it is beautiful."

Benicio gestured to the others. "Please, have a seat."

Brooke and Mark found a chair while Isabella remained standing studying the wealth of artifacts that the man had accumulated.

"Johann told me a little about what you are doing in Argentina. Looking for a U-boat? Yes?"

Brooke nodded. "Yes. We believe it has a connection to something we found in Germany."

"We're only interested in the one. It was said to have gone up the river," Mark explained.

"Ah, yes. The U-2853."

Mark's eyes widened with sudden excitement. "It existed? You have a number?"

Benicio nodded. "Of course."

"How—how did you find a number?"

Benicio smiled. "You my friend, are in for a treat."

Mark frowned and looked questioningly at Brooke. She shrugged. "Don't look at me."

"What do you mean?" Mark asked Benicio.

"I'm about to take you to talk to a man who was on that submarine. Providing he is still alive."

"You're kidding!" Mark exclaimed.

"No, my friend, I certainly am not."

———

Franz Otto was a man in his nineties, and while his mind seemed like it was still young, his body appeared to be failing him in his later years. The group congregated in his living room which was decorated sparsely. However, a painting of a German U-boat looked as though it took pride of place on the wall behind his lounge chair.

He looked at them all and asked in a raspy voice, *"Was schulde ich dem Vergnügen?"* What do I owe the pleasure?

Brooke looked at Mark who replied in German, "We are here to ask about your boat?"

"I do not have a boat," he replied in English.

Mark smiled. "You speak English."

"And you speak Deutsche."

"Can I ask you about U-2853?"

The old man nodded.

"When did you arrive in Argentina?"

"March Twenty-Seven."

Mark hesitated. "Why did your U-boat come here?"

"To deliver our cargo."

"What cargo?"

Otto said, "We had passengers and crates."

"Do you know what was in them?"

"No."

"Who were the passengers?"

"Party officials."

A surge of adrenaline ran through Mark. "I heard the submarine went up the river. Where did it go?"

"I don't know," Otto replied without guile.

Mark frowned. "You don't know?"

"I was not on it. The Kapitan allowed some of us to remain behind. For us, the war was over. We were not going back."

"Did the U-boat come back down the river?"

Otto shook his head. "No."

"What happened to it then?"

"I do not know."

"Do you think it's possible that they went to New Hope?" Brooke asked.

Otto shrugged. "It is possible, I guess. I have heard that there were Germans there."

"Did any more U-boats come to Buenos Aires?" Mark asked.

Otto shook his head. "Only the three."

Yes, the three. Mark had forgotten about those. "What did the others come for?"

"I heard they were unloaded at night onto boats which took whatever they were carrying up the river."

Otto sighed, he looked tired.

"I have one final question if that is all right?" Mark asked.

The old man nodded.

"Did any stolen treasure come to Argentina?"

"I do not know."

"Could there have been some in the crates you brought on the U-2853?"

"It is possible, I guess."

Mark nodded. "Thank you, Mister Otto. It has been great to talk to you."

"I'm afraid I wasn't able to help much."

Mark nodded. "You helped more than you know, sir."

From their concealed position across the road, the watchers observed the group leaving the old German's home. They'd tracked them from the airport to San Isidro, and then to their destination here.

"Now what do you suppose they were doing there?" their leader, Egon Bach asked no one in particular.

Bach had been chosen to lead by Heinrich Wolfsjunge because of his looks and experience. He was in his late twenties, had blond hair, and was solidly built. He'd served with the German armed forces before being discharged after refusing an order from a dark-skinned officer. He wasn't out of work for long, however, for it was just after that he'd been approached by Wolfsjunge.

"According to my search a man named Franz Otto lives here," Georg Forst said.

Bach looked at his thin counterpart. "Who is Franz Otto? He sounds German."

"Shall we go and find out?" Forst asked.

"I believe we should."

Parana River, Argentina

After spending three days on the river, searching and coming up empty, the group was tired and rather frustrated. Actually, all had been that way since the day before except Mark, who found everything to be quite the adventure. However, by the end of the third day he too was starting to feel it. They pulled their small boat onto a grass-covered riverbank for the night and began to discuss their options. Brooke said, "We should go to La Cumbrecita tomorrow."

In the lantern light the group appeared dejected, having failed to find anything at all. Mark shook his head, unwilling to admit defeat. "It must be there. It can't just have vanished."

"We've been up and down how many times, and still found nothing," Brooke pointed out.

Garcia took out his map, unfolded it, and said, "We could stop at Rosario and go inland from there."

Mark saw Brooke grimace. "You know you shouldn't fold maps, right?"

Garcia shrugged.

"Is there anyone in Rosario we could talk to?" Mark asked.

"I will think upon it," the guide commented and stared out into the darkness.

Mark frowned and put his hand out. "Could I have a look at your map, please?"

Garcia nodded and passed it to him. In the dim light, Mark studied it while the others talked amongst themselves. The sounds of the night seemed to ebb and flow. The frogs were the loudest.

"Son of a—"

They all looked at Mark, whose eyes were big and round. He looked up at Garcia. "How old is this map?"

"Nineteen forty-eight I think, why?"

Mark dug into his pack and took out his own map. He spread it out on the ground and lay the other one beside it. "Look."

Brooke detected the difference immediately, having been in the military and relying on maps herself a lot it was easy. "The course of the river is different."

"Yes," said Mark. "We're looking in the wrong place. How far do you figure it's changed, Brooke?"

"Five-hundred meters, maybe. You know, for a pain in the butt you're reasonably smart."

He smiled at her. "I have to earn my keep somehow. The big bucks I'm getting paid."

She glared at him. "I take that back."

"It's only in the one place," Garcia pointed out. "It could have changed course through a flood. There was a large one in nineteen fifty-three which could account for the river shift. But I've been past that area many times, the jungle there is very thick."

"It's a good thing I brought along something we could use then, isn't it?" Mark said smugly.

"I thought I told you to leave that thing behind," Brooke snapped.

"You did," he said, feeling vindicated in his decision.

"Uh, huh," she grunted rolling her eyes.

"I've got a drone which should do the trick," Mark explained.

"Cool," Isabella said with a smile. Then, "Why have you got a drone?"

"He's a teenage boy in a man's body; why do you think?" Brooke said mockingly.

Isabella raised her eyebrows. "Oh."

"That's not true," Mark growled. "It's a hobby of mine. I thought it might come in handy. Looks like I was right."

"We'll see," Brooke said.

"If it works, you can buy me dinner." The suggestion was almost a challenge.

She coughed. "I don't think so."

Five minutes later, they were back on the water and traveling upstream.

8

THE JUNGLE OF DEATH

Parana River, Argentina

Mark worked the controls and the DJI Mavic 2 Pro drone lifted quickly into the heavy humid air. He watched the feed coming to the screen of his cell before him. The drone rose above the thick forest of trees, and he paused it for a moment, keeping it in a hover and maneuvering the camera so he could scan the area and ensure all was in working order before sending it further afield.

"Everything seems fine," he allowed. "I'll keep going."

Soon the drone disappeared behind the trees, and he flew using the camera as a guide. Mark worked in a grid pattern, covering one area before moving on to the next. With the drone high enough, it was possible to see the old watercourse which he noticed was almost totally overgrown.

There were patches of water where the old channel was deeper than the other areas. The waterway twisted and turned for the three miles the drone followed it. "I can't see anything," Mark said. "The canopy is too thick."

"Can you get lower?" Brooke asked.

"I can try," he replied. "I'll turn it around and come back."

Mark dropped the drone lower and retraced the flight path back the other way. Suddenly Garcia's eyes widened. "Wait, I see something."

"Where?" Mark asked.

"Circle back. There was some water in a deep channel where the tree canopy parted for just an instant and I thought I saw something."

Mark did as he was asked and circled the drone back the opposite way.

Garcia said, "You'll see it in a moment."

Up ahead the tree canopy parted, and Mark caught sight of some water. "Okay, it looks like we've found the opening. How about I take it down for a closer look?"

The drone dipped and flew down through the hole in the canopy. The picture darkened but Mark adjusted it until it cleared.

"Oh, my," Isabella said. "Is that what I think it is?"

An object filled the screen and was covered in debris from years of sitting idle, but the outline was unmistakable. They were looking at a Type XXI U-boat.

"Now all we have to do is get to it," Brooke said.

———

The jungle was dense and the insects that bred in the damp earth were almost on par with the undergrowth. The smell of rotting vegetation was profuse in the humid air. Mark slapped at his neck where he'd been bitten for the hundredth time. Behind him came Isabella, who was followed by Garcia. Brooke led the way through the wall of green. A branch whipped back and smacked Mark across his right cheek, leaving a small welt in its wake.

The light was dappled under the canopy and made it difficult to make out raised roots creating a trip hazard. Then something occurred to Mark. "I hope we don't see any snakes."

"Which ones in particular?" Brooke asked.

"Rattlesnakes, Pit Vipers, and Fer de Lance. Ones that'll kill you. Oh and don't forget the yellow anacondas in the northeast love the swampy areas."

Behind him, Isabella said, "You had to bring it to the forefront of everybody's mind, didn't you?"

"Helps to be prepared," Mark replied.

"Great," Isabella said, giving his shoulder a gentle push.

He kept after Brooke, and they soon came to the old river. The banks dropped down to the bed which was covered in branches and debris. Brooke slid down and turned left to follow the old course. She'd gone half a mile before she reached a twist in the riverbed and disappeared around it, and Mark lost sight of her.

Not for long though as he made the turn himself. He saw her stopped in front of him and then noticed the reason what she'd come to an abrupt halt. All 250 feet of U-boat. He trudged up to stand beside her. "Wow."

"You've got that right," Brooke said. "Wow is so an accurate description."

The U-boat rested on the bottom of the old riverbed surrounded by a large pool of putrid looking, scum-covered water. It was almost concealed in debris, its number still visible, although faded.

"Of all the times I have traveled this river, and I never knew that it was here," Garcia said as he joined the pair, disbelief on his face and in the tone of his voice.

"It's amazing," gasped Isabella.

Mark looked around. "I wonder how deep the water is."

Brooke said, "There is a lean on the boat so it must be sitting on the bottom. I figure no deeper than your waist."

"Alright, let's do this," suggested Mark, rubbing his hands together as though impatient to get on board.

Isabella wrinkled her nose and nodded towards the stagnant water. "Through that?"

"It's the only way by the looks of it," Mark said.

"You go first," Brooke said.

"All right," Mark replied, putting down his pack.

"Before you go ahead, Indiana Jones, let's just try something first."

Mark looked curiously at Brooke. "You want to go ahead of me?"

"Patience, man," Brooke said and bent down to pick up a stick. She tossed it into the air, and they all followed the arc until it hit the water with a light splash.

The water erupted in a violent maelstrom, green and surging, exposing the savage killers lurking beneath it. Mark's eyes widened as he realized that he would have been walking to his death, ripped apart by the caimans hidden below the surface.

"That could have been me." The words were almost distant. "So, our first option is out of the question. How are we going to get over there now?"

"That, dear Mark, is the question."

"I have found something that might possibly work," Isabella told them as she walked back from further along the old riverbed. They had split up, intent on finding anything which might give them access across the stinking water filled with Jurassic death. "I must stress might though."

"What did you find?" Brooke asked her, turning to face in her direction.

"A boat. Maybe boat is the wrong description – it's more of a dinghy actually."

"We'd better have a look at it," Brooke told her.

They retraced Isabella's steps along the riverbed until they reached it. Mark shook his head in wonderment. "If that thing floats, I'm Albert Einstein."

The small vessel was wooden, and by the look of it had been there for as long as the river had been diverted. The timbers were rotting, and there were several holes in the bottom, albeit not big ones, but holes none the less. There was even an oar. Half an oar, anyway.

"I did say might," Isabella reminded them.

"It'll work," Brooke told them.

"What year?" asked Mark. "The thing will sink, and we'll become caiman burgers."

Brooke shrugged. "While they're eating you, I'll be able to get aboard."

"Fantastic."

"Look, the holes aren't that big. The distance to the U-boat is short. Chances are we won't even sink by the time we get there."

"What if you're wrong?"

She smiled broadly. "Been interesting knowing you, buddy."

"Great, just great."

―――――

They moved the dinghy along the riverbed to the edge of the water without too much fuss. Putting it in at the shore caused an immediate reaction by a couple of caimans that attacked the side of it. Mark looked at Brooke and shrugged, saying, "Maybe they'll eat the boat instead of us."

"Get in," she told him. "I'll paddle."

"What do you want us to do if it goes wrong?" Garcia asked.

"Put flowers on my grave," Mark said drily.

"Get in the boat, Mark," Brooke ordered. "You're starting to annoy me."

He climbed in, the rocking motion attracting more attention from the caimans. Water began seeping into the bottom of the vessel through the little holes. Brooke followed him in and with a push of the oar the dinghy moved away from safety.

Almost immediately the water around them became a turbulent and roiling mass as the reptiles started to gravitate towards the wooden boat. Two launched themselves at it, one taking a piece out of the edge. Mark jumped at the animal's ferocity.

"Hang on, we're almost there," Brooke said. "Did you bring the rope?"

"It's in my pack."

"Get it out."

The dinghy stopped just forward of the conning tower. Brooke put the oar down and said, "Pass me the rope."

Mark handed it over, aware that the water in the bottom of the dinghy was now up to his ankles. For small holes they sure let in a lot of water.

Brooke hastily made a loop at the end of the rope like a lariat. She then started to twirl it above her head and threw it toward the U-boat's long topside deck. The rope slid back down, almost catching on some of the overgrowth, before dropping into the water beside the dinghy. A caiman grasped at it with powerful jaws, but

Brooke was a touch quicker than the reptile, and pulled it aboard.

"What are you doing?" Mark asked impatiently.

"On the deck there will be some cleat-looking things that they used to tie the submarine to the dock. I forget what they're actually called. We need to get past some of this brush and with a bit of luck I can lasso one of them, then we pull ourselves up there."

"Then I suggest you hurry up."

Brooke looked down and saw the depth of the water. It wouldn't be long and the dinghy would sink, leaving them at the mercy of the caimans.

She tried again and missed. "Shit."

"John Wayne you ain't, little sister," Mark said in a low drawl.

"Shut up." She drew her Glock and passed it to Mark. "Here, just in case one of our hungry friends gets over ambitious."

Mark took the weapon and made sure there was a round in the chamber.

Brooke tried a third time and missed again, the rope trailing a large branch.

"You really suck at this, Brooke," Mark said nervously.

"You want me to push you out of the boat?"

"Not particularly."

"Then put a sock in it."

The water in the bottom of the boat had increased alarmingly. There were caimans nudging up to the side, and Brooke was still pretending she was a cowgirl.

Swing and a miss.

"I don't mean to add any pressure, Brooke, but our friends are looking awfully hungry."

Another miss.

Mark chuckled sarcastically. "I hope you have enough bullets in this thing."

"Got it."

He looked up and saw Brooke tugging at the rope, making sure it was secure. She looked at him and grinned. "Follow me."

They climbed up the side of the U-boat, pushing aside the overgrowth as they went, and made it to the deck. Mark looked back down in time to see the dinghy slide beneath the water with two caimans in it. "I guess we won't be going back that way."

"Come on," Brooke said, "let's find a way in."

———

It smelled damp and musty and old. Years of contained air without a ventilation system running and circulating it throughout the boat hadn't done it any favors. However, having been sealed for as long as it had been, it was a time capsule, and they were stepping back in time.

They managed to get into the conning tower and from there, down into the boat itself. Brooke led the way through the underwater beast until they found what appeared to be the captain's cabin.

It was cozy—codeword for cramped. There was a small table against the bulkhead and a cot along the one opposite the hatch where they entered. "Look," said Mark pointing at the captain's table. Sitting on it was what appeared to be a small book.

Brooke picked it up and opened it. "It looks like a diary. I can't tell because it's written in German."

"But you speak German," Mark pointed out.

She passed him the book. "Barely. Enough to get by."

Mark looked through it.

...now been at sea for fifteen days with no sight of enemy activity...

...today we go up the river. The water is higher than usual which will make our passage easier...

...we shall be rid of our passengers today. I for one will not be sorry to see them gone...

...the last of the crew and myself will leave today for Neue Hoffnung. I hope that our lives will be better now that we have reached our new home. Once things settle then maybe we can bring our families to the new land...

That was where the entries ended.

"You're right, it is a diary. It looks like it catalogued their trip here to Argentina. It mentions passengers and about hoping to bring the crew's families here to New Hope."

"Does it mention artifacts or anything like that?"

"I don't know."

"Keep looking, I'll go through the rest of the U-boat and see what I can find."

Mark flicked through it again to see if there was any mention of the treasure being unloaded. He found nothing and frowned. Then he chastised himself for being foolish and not looking towards the front for any mention of it being loaded. He found one passage and it wasn't what he expected.

...waiting for five hours for the cargo to arrive and still there is nothing. We have been here long enough. It is time to sail. The longer we wait, the more dangerous it becomes, and we will be putting to sea in daylight...

"They never took on the cargo," Mark muttered to himself. "It never arrived."

If Webster was right and there was never any treasure

in Portugal except for the gold, and there wasn't any on the U-boat, then—

"Well Sherlock, what did you find? I came up with nothing except a few old machineguns."

He looked at her wide-eyed. Brooke could see he was troubled. "What is it?"

"The captain sailed without the cargo. It never arrived."

"You're sure?"

"It says it right here in the book. "Listen—waiting for five hours for the cargo to arrive and still there is nothing. We have been here long enough. It is time to sail. The longer we wait, the more dangerous it becomes, and we will be putting to sea in daylight—he sailed without it."

"That's interesting."

"Nothing in Portugal, nothing on the U-boat, I'm going to take a wild stab and say the *Wilhelm Gustloff* didn't have anything on it as well."

"What happened to it all then? Where is the room that was mentioned?"

"Both good questions," Mark replied.

"I think we should go to New Hope and look around."

"There is no point," Mark said. "We should go back to Berlin and start again, looking at it in a different way."

"What different way?"

"Trying to find out where it went after it left where the Nazis were storing it."

"Isn't that what we were trying to do?"

Mark shook his head. "No, we're looking at destinations."

Brooke sighed. "You're like him, you know?"

"Who?"

"Your father. You and he are like two peas in a pod."

"I'm nothing like him," Mark retorted with more than a hint of bitterness in his voice.

"You are. And soon enough you'll realize it. Mind I think he might've been a little smarter than you. He listened to things he was told."

"You mean from you?"

Brooke smiled. "Of course. Maybe you'll take a leaf from his book one day. It'll happen, mark my words."

"Whatever."

Brooke glared at him.

"Sorry, were we having a moment?"

"It was not a moment."

"I thought we must have been the way you reacted," he teased.

"Oh, grow up."

"Should we leave now?" Mark asked.

Brooke nodded. "Yes. Johann will be most disappointed."

"We still made a good find," Mark pointed out. He held up the diary. "This might yield something yet."

"Follow me," Brooke said.

———

"This got bad real fast," Brooke said as she rested her hand on the butt of the Glock behind her back. They stood on the deck outside and stared across the small expanse of water to where they had left Garcia and Isabella. Only it wasn't just those two anymore. They'd been joined by three men, who were armed and looked dangerous.

"Who do you think they are?" Mark asked.

"Hello, Mark, Brooke," one of the men greeted them. His accent was thick and unmistakably German.

"I guess he knows who we are," Mark said.

"It would seem so," Brooke agreed.

"Would you care to join us?" Forst asked.

"Not particularly," Brooke called back to him.

"It was not a request."

Mark had an idea. "Why don't you all come over here and get us."

Brooke looked at him. "You know—"

"I do."

Bach gestured to their third man, Fischer who started forward. Mark said in a low voice, "This is not going to be pretty."

"When it happens get back inside," Brooke told him.

"Yes, ma'am."

Fischer had only taken a few steps into the murky water when it churned to life. He stopped suddenly, confused, then by the time he figured he was in trouble, it was too late.

A caiman came out of the water, its jaws wide. Fischer let out a shriek as the reptile fastened onto his leg above the knee. Another appeared and grabbed the other leg and before he knew it, Fischer was being pulled into the water.

"Go!" Brooke snapped and they ran back the way they'd come.

On the dry riverbed, Bach and Forst opened fire with their weapons at the seething water as they tried to help their friend.

Seeing that their captors were distracted, Isabella and Garcia took off into the jungle to hide.

Bach and Forst ran to the edge of the water to see if there was anything they could do, but their comrade was gone. All they could see was a large patch of red boiling up from the foaming water.

Forst looked around. "Where did they go?"

Bach followed his gaze. "Blast. Go and look for them. I'll keep an eye on the submarine."

Forst headed into the thick jungle, searching for Isabella and Garcia. Meanwhile on the U-boat, Brooke and Mark were formulating a plan.

———

"Here, hold this," Mark said thrusting a weapon into Brooke's arms.

"What are you doing?" she asked. "I haven't seen one of these before."

"Cool, something I can teach you. German made MG42 machinegun," Mark said opening another box. "It is capable of firing a thousand rounds per minute. Should give our friends something to think about."

"Do you think it will work after all this time?"

Mark took an ammunition belt from the box he'd just opened. He then flipped open the belt feed mechanism and pointed at some stuff inside. "See that, it still has grease in it. It'll work. If anything, the ammunition might play up."

Grabbing the MG42 from her, Mark loaded it then gathered another belt and forced it into Brooke's hands before hanging the machinegun over his shoulders by the strap.

As soon as he emerged onto the deck of the U-boat, Mark opened fire. The MG42 rattled through the first belt as though it were a starving metal beast, unfed for the whole 75 years it had been secured away in the crate.

Bach dove behind an old deadfall tree long exposed with the subsidence of the water level over the years. Bullets chewed into the log sending wicked splinters scything through the air.

When the machinegun fell silent, Mark snapped, "Give me the other belt."

Careful not to touch anything near the barrel because of the weapon's excessive heat, he reloaded and prepared to fire again.

Bach leaped to his feet and fired at the pair on the U-boat. Getting out of the line of fire, Brooke dived for the deck, but Mark showed a coolness she hadn't seen from him until now. He snapped the belt feeder shut and opened fire once more.

Forst appeared out of the jungle, drawn by the cacophony of the weapon's fire. He stopped suddenly as he was confronted with Bach running towards him, dirt kicking up at his heels from the impact of the bullets.

"Run!" he shouted. "Get out of here."

Forst turned and ran as fast as he could, the pair disappearing into the jungle with bullets chewing down vegetation behind them like a hungry herbivorous dinosaur.

Mark stopped firing. His eyes scanned the jungle as they looked for the two men. When he was satisfied they were gone, he turned to Brooke and asked, "Are you okay?"

"Where have you been hiding that guy?" she asked.

"I try to keep him locked up. Stupid things seem to happen when he comes out."

There was movement from the jungle and Brooke reached for her Glock, lowering it again and sighing with relief at the sight of Isabella and Garcia stepping out into the open. "It's only us," Isabella called out.

"Are you alright?"

"We're fine. What about you?"

"We're all good."

"Stay there, we'll be over shortly," Brooke said. Then

quietly so only her and Mark could hear, "Just as soon as we figure out how."

Mark said, "You ever see those cartoons where they run along the backs of the crocodiles to reach the riverbank?"

Brooke looked at him curiously. "Yeah, sure."

He smiled. The old Mark was back. "Count that out."

She scowled at him. "You see the one where the woman with the gun shoots the pain in her backside and pushes him into the water so the caimans can eat him?"

"I'm guessing we're not going to do that either, right?"

Brooke gave him a mirthless smile. "It's an option I'm seriously considering."

The water was still boiling from where the reptiles were fighting over the corpse beneath the surface. Maybe the thrashing around would attract all of them and they could get over on the other side.

Brooke walked across the deck and looked down. She could see nothing, which didn't mean that they weren't there lurking in the murky water. She bent down and picked up part of a broken branch from the deck. "Here goes nothing."

She dropped it into the water and the reaction was immediate. The water exploded as a single, much larger caiman thrashed out. Mark stood beside her and said, "On the positive side, there's only one of them on this side."

"Which also happens to be the father of all caimans. It's mighty big." Brooke sighed.

She looked around then up. "All right, we'll have to do it that way."

"What way?"

"Get the rope in the tree and swing across to the bank."

"Like Tarzan?"

"Something like that."

Mark nodded again. "What do we do?"

"We test out my cowgirl skills again."

"Good grief."

"Is that a complaint I hear?"

Mark held up both hands. "No, ma'am. Cowgirl up."

"Get the rope."

Mark came back with the rope and Brooke went to work with it. After only a couple of goes the rope got hooked up on a branch. Brooke tested it and it seemed fine. Then she tied the MG42 to the end of it.

"What's with that?" Mark asked.

"The rope won't be heavy enough to swing back up here after you get off so the extra weight should help."

"Okay, but why do I get to go first? I always ascribed to the notion of ladies before gentlemen. Not claiming to be a gentleman by any stretch, but you get the gist."

"You scared?"

Mark gave her an indignant look. "Me? Scared? No, not in the least. We did obstacle course training in the military. This will be child's play. What's the worst that could happen?"

"Don't let the nasty caiman eat you."

Mark rolled his eyes. "I'm sure he's down there thinking, I hope Brooke don't open a can of whoop ass on me and turn me into a handbag."

Brooke handed him the rope. "I would be if I were him. Now, let's go."

Mark took hold of the rope. "If I die, I'm coming back to—"

She pushed him.

With a shout of alarm and surprise, Mark left the deck of the U-boat. He dropped towards the water until the rope snapped taut and then started to swing towards the dry land of the old riverbed, skimming just above the murky liquid.

His feet touched dry land and he felt a wave of relief wash over him. Mark looked back at Brooke and saw there was as much relief on her face as there possibly was on his. "Piece of cake," he called back.

"Told you it would be," she replied. "Now, swing it back to me."

Mark swung the rope. The weight of the machinegun took it back all the way and Brooke caught it up at the end of its arc.

Mark watched her prepare herself for the swing. She stepped out and dropped towards the water.

Then all those on dry land watched on in horror as the rope broke and Brooke plunged into the water.

———

Mark never hesitated. He picked up a solid branch at his feet and with Isabella's cries of alarm ringing in his ears, he launched himself into the water.

As soon as he landed, Mark began wildly thrashing at the water's surface with the branch. The caiman had already surfaced with the entry of Brooke and was headed towards his prey, his powerful tail closing the distance in an instant.

The caiman's jaws opened wide as it readied itself to grab Brooke about her waist. Had it done so the force would have crushed her lower ribs and punctured any number of vital organs. But as it was, Mark's violent intervention with the branch managed to distract it.

The beast turned and started towards him, and he suddenly realized that his actions had placed him in danger.

A quick glance told him that Brooke was muddy but

out of peril, so he started moving backward, not taking his eyes from the approaching reptile.

The beast came closer with every powerful swish of its tail. Mark tried to hurry but his movement through the water was akin to a bad dream, being chased by a snake but you can't run away quick enough.

"This was a bad idea, Mark. You had to play the hero," he said out loud to himself.

The water had soaked his clothes and they felt like lead weights holding him back. Safety was just there, a few small steps away; if he could just go a little quicker. Come on, move.

The massive beast's jaws opened wide, its tail flicked, and as it leaped forward, Mark closed his eyes as he threw himself backward, missing the bank and landing in the muddy water.

CRACK, CRACK, CRACK!

Mark's eyes flew open in time to see the caiman roll over in the water, a pool of red already starting to spread around it. He looked beyond it to see Brooke standing clear of the water holding her Glock. She said, "Are you getting out or staying there? You know just in case the others come back."

Nodding vigorously, he stood up dripping fetid water and lunged towards the edge of the pool and pulled himself clear. Dropping to his knees, he sucked in great gulps of air as he turned to see how close he'd come to being caiman food.

Isabella knelt beside Mark and wrapped her arms around him. "That was so brave," she whispered into his ear. "You are a hero, Marco. Are you alright?"

He nodded and climbed to his feet after she let him go. "I'm fine, thanks to Brooke."

Brooke joined them, her wet clothes clung to her, and she looked to be a little shaken. Before she said anything, she wrapped her arms around him, pulling him close to her. He tried to laugh his discomfort off. "Two ladies in my arms in a min—"

"Just shut up," Brooke said to him. "Thank you, you saved my life."

"As you did mine."

"That's the way it's meant to be in a team," she said and let him go. "Now, shall we get out of here?"

Mark's eyes widened, remembering something. "Oh, no, the diary."

He reached inside his shirt and took it out. Water-logged and all but falling apart. "Blast it, Brooke, I'm sorry."

"It's all right. You read some of it. Who knows, maybe Greg can do something with it when we get back."

"We are headed back to Berlin?" Isabella asked.

"Yes. There was nothing on the U-boat," Brooke explained. "There never was."

9

THE PAUPER'S GRAVE

Berlin, Germany

Johann Schmidt looked at his team as they sat around the conference table. His gaze settled on Mark, Brooke, and Isabella. "It is good to have you back safely. I only wish the news were better."

"It wasn't a total loss," Brooke said. "We found out that there was nothing on the U-boat."

Schmidt nodded grimly. "Which makes me wonder about the *Wilhelm Gustloff*."

"I say there was nothing on it either," Mark said voicing his opinion.

"That could well be, Mister Butler," Schmidt agreed. "However, if that is the case, what became of the Amber Room?"

"There is something else we need to pay attention to as well," Brooke pointed out. "The men who came after us knew where we were as well as calling us by name."

"What are you saying, Brooke?" Schmidt asked.

"Nothing yet, but I'd like to know how they did. And I aim to find out."

"Yes, I agree; look into it. Now, the diary which was brought back from Argentina." He looked at Turow.

"I did what I could, but it was almost beyond help. The swim it took did it no favors."

Mark felt like defending his actions but remained silent.

Turow continued. "I'm not blaming you, Mark. What you did was an act of selflessness. It is a trait I wish more people had these days."

"Was there anything you discovered that might be of use?" Schmidt asked.

"The only thing I found was a reference to the Six-Hundred and First Pioniere Battalion. I wasn't able to make anything else out."

The German billionaire looked at Werner Krause. "Does anything come to mind, Mister Krause?"

"The Six-Hundred and First Pioniere Battalion was formed in late December of nineteen forty-four. They were to be a combat engineer battalion but with the Soviets closing in so fast to the east, and the fact that they had a full complement of trucks, they were used for other things."

"By other things do you mean transporting artifacts?"

Krause shrugged. "It is all unclear. Perhaps, I'm not sure. Many things we learn about the end of the war are not documented so well."

Schmidt looked at Molly. "Can you work with Werner and see what you can find out?"

"Yes, sir."

Mark cleared his throat.

"What is it, Mister Butler?"

"We're forgetting one thing."

"What might that be?"

"We should be looking further into Gerhard Wolff. Remember in the diary of Hans Becker, Wolff ordered them to Austria and Lake Toplitz. What if he changed all of their orders at the last minute?"

"Werner and Molly—"

"Werner and Molly are busy. What about Brooke and I?"

Schmidt looked at Brooke and raised his eyebrows questioningly. "Brooke?"

Her nod was almost imperceptible.

"All right then, Mister Butler, you and Brooke can look into it; see what you can find. Mister Webster will set you up in the database and you can start there. Mister Webster, once you've finished there, I want you to find out who those men in Argentina were."

"It'll be like looking for the proverbial needle in a darn haystack," he complained quietly to himself.

"If the job is too big—"

"I never said that," Webster interrupted his boss.

"Okay, then let's get started."

———

Germany

"Once again you have failed me," Wolfsjunge said plainly. "How many times is that, Egon?"

Bach looked at the floor. "I'm sorry, sir. They—"

"I do not want excuses. I want results."

"Yes, sir."

"By now they know that the artifacts were not on the U-boat. Which means that they will assume there was nothing aboard the ship when it sailed." There was fire in Wolfsjunge's eyes and Bach suddenly felt anxious.

"Sir—"

"My source tells me that they are now going to focus

on Gerhard Wolff. You had one mission in Argentina and now—argh! I have no words."

"We tried—"

"Excuses! What did I say? Undoubtedly, they will find out that Gerhard was the one behind the disappearance of the treasure. And not only will they find that out, but they will then keep looking, and looking, and looking, and looking. It is something I do not need when we are this close to finding it ourselves. I must have that *room*!"

"The room, sir?"

"Yes, the room. The Amber Room, you fool. What use is having all of the treasure if I cannot have the jewel in the crown?"

There was a knock at the door and a tall, dark-haired woman entered. "You wanted to see me, sir?"

"Yes, Anika. I was just in the process of telling Mister Bach he's fired."

"Understood, sir," Anika Meyer said, took out a Glock 19, and shot Bach where he stood.

Berlin, Germany

Mark leaned back in his seat and let out a long sigh. He rubbed at his eyes and said, "How many hours is that we've been at it?"

Brooke looked at her wristwatch. "A little over five. Go and have a rest."

Mark sat up again. "No, I'll be fine. Just have square eyes once we're done. I wish we could find something useful."

"We know things," Brooke reminded him. "We know that after the end of the war, Wolff was tried at Nuremburg. He did ten years in prison before he was released and went to Munich in Bavaria."

Mark took over the narrative, "Where he remained, according to our files, until nineteen fifty-seven. He lived alone and like a pauper. After which there is no record of him. Surely if you had all of that treasure you'd be living in relative comfort."

Brooke thought for a moment. "It's strange."

"Sure, it is. All that treasure—"

"No. The fact that he just disappeared. There is no record of him anywhere after fifty-seven. He was only out of prison two years and then he seemed to disappear into thin air. Why?"

"He died," Mark said with a shrug of his shoulders.

"Exactly."

Suddenly, Mark was interested once more. "But if he died, wouldn't there be a record of it?"

"Maybe someone didn't want a record of it," Brooke said.

"You mean someone killed him?"

"It's possible. But remember, the war had only been over for twelve years. It was still raw. He lived a pauper's lifestyle, maybe he died and was given a pauper's grave."

"Wouldn't they still have a record of it, though?"

"Not a public one. But if anyone knows where to look, then it would be Werner or Greg."

Mark stood up; all his fatigue had fallen away. "Let's go and find out."

Brooke smiled at him. "All right, we'll try Werner."

———

Krause and Molly looked like Mark had felt not more than fifteen minutes before. When Molly saw him approaching with Brooke she smiled. "Rescue me."

"How goes it?" Mark asked.

"It's like poking broken matches into my eyes," Molly growled.

"It's not that bad," Krause said.

Molly held her hand up to her face pretending that Krause couldn't see her. She nodded and mouthed, "Yes, it is."

"I can see you, you know?"

"I gather you haven't had any luck thus far?" Brooke asked.

"Nothing," Krause replied. "We thought we might be able to find someone who was part of the Pioniere Battalion and be able to ask them questions."

"We keep coming to a dead end," Molly said. "Literally."

Mark tried hard not to smile, and Krause growled, "Not funny, Molly."

"Werner," Brooke started, "where is the best place to find records of a pauper's grave in Munich?"

Krause frowned. "Why?"

"We have a theory we want to check out."

He looked thoughtful for a moment. "Hmm. There is a place I can think of. I'll text you the name and address, so you have a copy on your cell."

"Thanks. We'll go and see Johann. Good luck."

"You, too."

When they reached Schmidt's office, Brooke knocked briefly before entering without waiting for a reply. The foundation head was looking over papers and when he saw who it was, he stopped and beckoned with his hand that they come in, before asking, "Did you find something?"

"A theory," Brooke told him.

"What theory?"

She told him about the discussion she and Mark had had. Schmidt nodded. "It's quite feasible I suppose. All right, take the company jet. Let me know what you find."

———

Germany

"They have gone to Munich," Anika Meyer told her boss.

"What for?"

"Looking for records into paupers' graves."

"Why would they be doing that, I wonder?" the man mused out loud.

"What do you want me to do?" She stood awaiting his orders.

"Have someone keep an eye on them. Find out what they're doing."

"Do you want me to kill them?"

Wolfsjunge shook his head. "No, if Schmidt and his people are determined to find the treasure then we'll watch and wait. Let them perform the work for us."

"As you wish."

———

Munich

"Mister Vogel?" Brooke asked the bespectacled man behind the counter.

He raised his head and turned his tired eyes to take in the two people before him. "Yes?"

"My name is Brooke Reynolds, and this is Mark

Butler. We work for the Schmidt Foundation. Maybe you've heard of it?"

Vogel thought for a moment then nodded. "I think so."

"We search for lost relics across the globe."

"Treasure?" he asked.

"If you wish to call it that."

"What is it that I can help you with?"

"We understand that you have records of paupers' graves here. Is that correct?"

"Yes."

Brooke smiled at him. "If it's at all possible, would you be able to find some information for us from nineteen fifty-seven?"

"Do you have a name?"

"Gerhard Wolff."

The man froze. "I'm not familiar with that name."

"Mister Vogel, it is of the utmost importance that we at least try to find any information on this man." Brooke went on to tell him what they thought had happened to Wolff.

Vogel nodded. "It was commonplace for Nazi officers to be buried in paupers' graves after the war."

"Can you help us?"

The man sighed. "I'll try. Follow me."

They set off after the man who moved along a hallway and into a back room. It smelled of dust collected over many years. He walked along an isle of shelves and found a box. Vogel took it down and thrust it into the arms of Mark. "There. Good luck."

Mark turned away, about to be followed by Brooke, when Vogel said, "Not yet."

He took down another box and passed it to her. "These two boxes contain the names of all the Nazi officers who were buried in paupers' graves. If you don't find what you need in them, then I can't help you. The office closes in two hours." The man shuffled off, leaving them to their arduous and dusty task.

Brooke raised her eyebrows. "Thanks, I think."

_____

"Do you have any idea of how many Nazi officers were buried this way?" Mark stated.

Brooke rolled her eyes. "Hello, I'm going through this box."

"Right, sorry."

Sometime later, Vogel reappeared. "How is it going?"

"Nothing so far," Mark said.

"You need to bear in mind that a lot of them weren't buried under their own name."

Brooke stopped and stared at Mark. She could see the pained expression on his face. "Good grief. We're going to need to start again."

"I'm closing soon," Vogel reminded them.

Mark looked at Brooke. "How are we going to find him without his proper name?"

She looked at Vogel. "The ones with different names. Did they keep their original birthdates?"

"I assume so."

"I'll make a call," Mark said and took out his cell.

After a few rings, a voice said, "Hello, luv."

"Molly, I could really use your help."

"Anything for you."

"Can you send me Gerhard Wolff's birthdate?"

"Sure. Give me a minute."

"No probs."

"How's Munich?" Molly asked.

"Fine. How's life at the farm?"

Molly chuckled. "I see what you did there."

A few moments later. "The information should be hitting your cell now."

It pinged.

"Got it, thanks, Molly."

"Bye, luv."

Mark looked at the message on his cell.

"Well?" Brooke prompted.

"Twenty-fourth of November, nineteen oh two."

Brooke sighed. "Let's start again."

Mark rolled his eyes. "Yeah."

———

The first part of their mission was made simpler due to the dates and names on the front. They only needed November, so they put the appropriate ones with the corresponding date aside. The next part was trying to figure out which one was Wolff. A task made more difficult because there were eight files with the matching dates.

Vogel stood to one side and watched them anxiously. They were already an hour past his departure time but for some reason he never pushed the issue.

Mark laid out eight pieces of paper with details on them and took a picture with his cell. Then he sent it to Greg Turow but followed it up with a call.

"What do you want me to do with these?" Turow asked.

"Each one of these men was buried in a pauper's grave," Mark explained. "The dates match the birthdate of Gerhard Wolff. We're trying to work out if one of them was him."

"You think he was buried in a pauper's grave?"

"It would explain the way he disappeared in fifty-seven."

"This could take a while, you know that?"

"Yes. We're going to head back to Berlin tonight."

"All right. Come and see me first thing in the morning."

"Thanks, Greg," Mark said.

"I'm hopeful it'll lead to something."

————

Vogel breathed a sigh of relief when Brooke and Mark left, beginning to think he'd be stuck there all night. He walked out the office door and locked it behind him, stepping down onto the sidewalk and turning in the direction he walked every day after work was done. He took three steps, stopping as he almost bumped into a young woman with long dark hair. He looked up startled. "My apologies, fräulein. I did not see you."

The young woman smiled at him. It was a mirthless smile, and his reaction to seeing it was a shiver down his spine. "That is fine, Herr Vogel. It is you that I have come to see."

"I'm sorry, you'll have to come back tomorrow. I'm late."

Anika took out a handgun and gave him a sorrowful look. "I'm sorry, Herr Vogel, but you'll be a little later than expected."

————

Berlin, Germany

The next morning Mark and Brooke were in the office by eight. They found Turow at his desk, working as usual. He looked up at them, removing his glasses which he used often when doing computer work. "Good morning," he said jovially.

"It sounds like it could be," Brooke replied.

"Did you find something?" Mark asked with a hint of anticipation.

"I've narrowed your dead people down to two."

"Wow," Mark said. "How did you do that?"

"First off, three of them were actually the correct names. After that it got a little trickier. Each of the remaining five papers were signed by witnesses. So, I checked them. Three of the witnesses were actual people. I took a guess and thought maybe that the last couple names were composites. This part is beyond me, so I handed it off to Webster."

Mark felt disappointed that there were still no firm answers, and it must have shown on his face. Turow said, "If anyone can work that one, Webster can."

Mark nodded. "Great, thanks."

Brooke said, "Mark, why don't you go and check in with Webster while I have a quick talk with Greg."

"Okay," he said and walked off.

"What's up, Brooke?"

"I'm concerned."

"About what happened in Argentina?"

"Yes."

"Me too. Somehow whoever is responsible knows what we're doing."

"My thoughts too. The question is, how?" Brooke said.

"I don't like to say it, but could it be one of us?"

"Either that or the place is wired," Brooke theorized.

"You realize that it could be me," Turow said.

"It could be me, too, but it isn't. And I need to trust someone, and I figure you to be it."

"What do you want?"

"How good are your computer hacking skills?" she asked.

"Only just passable."

"Good, because mine suck. I need you to dig into everyone, even me."

"I can try."

"Thanks, Greg."

"Don't thank me yet. My hacking skills might just be as bad as yours."

———

Mark found Webster at his workstation, fingers dancing across the keyboard in front of him, eyes wide as they in turn danced across the screen. "Can I help you with something or are you just here to annoy me?"

"Greg gave you two names he thought might be composite to rundown. Do you have anything yet?"

"I might," Webster said arrogantly. "One name, the one I got a hit on, was Gerfried Sommer. I started with a search for the first and last name. That narrowed the field minimally. I won't bore you with the rest of what I did because you probably won't understand it, but when I was finished, I came up with the name Hilbert Sommer. I did a search into him and guess what?"

"What?" Brooke asked as she joined them.

"Hilbert Sommer was Gerhard Wolff's driver towards the end of the war."

"Who better to trust," Brooke said.

"He could have information about what happened to the three convoys," Mark said.

"He's dead," Webster informed them.

"There goes that."

"He does have a son, however," Webster said. "He lives in Berlin. His name is Isaak Sommer."

Mark looked at Brooke and smiled. "Could we be so lucky?"

"We'll find out, Indiana Jones. Come on. Webster, text me the address."

Webster screwed up his face. "Thanks, Webster. Great work, Webster, Webster you're a genius."

"I'll buy you dinner when we get back, Webster," Brooke said.

"Really?"

"No, but thanks."

"Yeah, right."

―――――――

"This is it," Brooke said pulling over to the curb on Oderstraße outside a small block of apartments. She cut the motor in the Mercedes GLS and opened the door to get out.

Mark looked at the cream-colored stucco on the building's exterior and said, "Should we have called ahead?"

Brooke shrugged. "Maybe."

They walked along the sidewalk to the entry and then up to the door. Brooke ran a finger down the names on the panel beside the entrance until she reached the one she needed and pressed the buzzer beside it. A moment later a voice said, "Hello?"

"Isaak Sommer?"

"Yes."

"My name is Brooke Reynolds. I work for the Schmidt Foundation here in Berlin. I was wondering if I might have a word, please."

A pause, then, "I'm sorry, I'm busy."

"It's about your father, Herr Sommer. I promise, it won't take up much of your time. You would really help the Foundation if you were to agree."

"Five minutes?"

"Yes, sir."

The door buzzed and Brooke pushed it open. She looked at Mark and said, "Step one complete."

———

Once they were inside the apartment, Brooke introduced herself once more and then Mark. "I'm sorry for the intrusion but what we discuss could really help out a lot."

Sommer pointed at a sofa against the wall in the cramped apartment. "Please, have a seat."

"Thank you."

Mark figured him to be around sixty, judging by the gray hair and lines upon his face. He scanned the room and saw some photos on a sideboard. One was of a woman holding a child. An image from another time. "That was my wife," Sommer said, noticing Mark's gaze. "Her and our son, Otto. They died not long after the picture was taken."

Mark suddenly felt bad for bringing attention to the memory. "Sorry."

"Tell me how I can help you."

"Your father was Hilbert Sommer?" Brooke asked.

"Yes."

"Mister Sommer. We believe that your father drove for Gerhard Wolff towards the end of the war," Mark said. "Is that true?"

Sommer hesitated slightly. "Yes, he did."

"Did he ever talk about the war?"

"Not really. He said it was a terrible time."

"Mister Sommer, we at the Schmidt Foundation are working to locate and repatriate priceless artworks and artifacts which were lost during the war. One in particular which happens to be the Amber Room. You've heard of it, right?"

He nodded. "Yes. But what does this have to do with my father?"

"Your father was Wolff's driver at the time the Nazis began desperately relocating the treasures towards the end of the war with the Russians advancing so rapidly. We were following leads pointing towards three convoys —truck convoys—trucks which never arrived at their destinations. Your father didn't happen to mention anything like this, did he?"

Again, a hesitation. "No."

"Are you sure?" asked Brooke.

"Quite sure."

"Could you tell us why your father signed paperwork for Wolff's pauper grave in nineteen fifty-seven?"

"He did what?"

"In fifty-seven when—well we assume that it is Wolff —when he died, he was buried in a pauper's grave. The paperwork was witnessed by Gerfried Sommer. Gerfried Sommer was actually your father. What we can't work out is why."

"I think I know," Mark said as he climbed from the sofa. He walked across the room and stopped in front of a painting on the wall. "What better place to hide a stolen artwork than in plain sight."

"I—I don't know what you mean."

"This painting here. Julian Falat's Widok Krakowa. Supposedly lost in nineteen forty-four. Now we find it here. It has to be worth a lot of money. Just the thing that could be used for a payment. Isabella is going to love this. Did Wolff give it to your father? I take it that your father was SS?"

The man's shoulders slumped. He nodded slowly. "Yes. It has been in my family since the end of the war."

Mark stared at him for a moment, certain he was still holding something back. "Mister Sommer, did your father keep a diary or anything like that throughout his war years."

Resignedly, Sommer came to his feet. "Wait here."

He was gone for a few minutes before emerging with a small box, placing it on a wooden coffee table between them before removing the lid.

Mark and Brooke leaned forward. Inside were a few items dating back to the time of the war. But what caught Mark's attention was the small book. Sommer reached in and took it out. He passed it to Mark who opened it and flicked through the pages.

10

THE TRAIN

Neustrelitz, Germany, 2nd February 1945

The night was bone-chilling cold. Hilbert Sommer stood near the Daimler-Benz G4 Staff Car watching the SS troops unloading the trucks and placing everything into the freight cars of the train. He'd lost count of how many trucks had come and gone but he recognized them all. He'd seen them as they had been loaded and left Carinhall.

The artworks and artifacts that had been intended to go to separate destinations were all here in one place being loaded. Once more a line of trucks pulled away, the vacated spaces quickly taken by the next in line. This one was loaded with larger crates. Heavier. He heard Wolff say, "I want them all loaded into a single freight car. Understood?"

A soldier saluted and hurried away. Wolff turned and walked towards Sommer. He stopped near the young SS-Unterscharführer and said, "Sergeant, you are witnessing something beyond your wildest imaginings. When

Germany rises from the ashes like the phoenix, all this wealth will fund the new Nazi party. It will be bigger and better than the one which we see crumbling before us. Already the framework is being assembled on the other side of the world. When the time is right, the Reich shall return."

Sommer straightened and his bootheels snapped together. "Sir."

"Never mind that, Hilbert. Is all in order for the train's arrival?"

"Yes, sir. The line into the mountains is clear."

Wolff nodded. "Good, good."

"What of the Reichsmarschall, Herr General?"

"What about him? He will squeal like a little pig but do nothing. Besides, once the enemy get their hands on him, he will most certainly hang or be shot."

A captain approached the two men. He passed Wolff a framed picture, saluted, and turned to hurry off. Wolff looked at Sommer and said, "This is for you, Hilbert. Take it. For being loyal and doing what I ask without question."

Sommer stiffened once more. "Thank you, General."

"You have earned it. But there is more. I have also decided to promote you. From now on you are a sturmbannführer. Congratulations, Herr Major."

"I—I don't know what to say. I am honored."

"It will be your job to make sure that after the war, the treasures are kept safe from discovery."

"But how, sir?"

"You will go with the train. I have hand-picked another man who will travel with you. There will also be a small escort. When you reach your destination the train crew and the escort must not be allowed to leave. Do you understand?"

Sommer frowned. "You want—"

"*Not* allowed to leave, Hilbert. The future of the new Reich depends on it."

"It will be done, Herr General. But what of you?"

"I am a resourceful man, Hilbert. I will get by after the war. You just concentrate on your mission."

"Jawohl, Herr Oberstgruppenführer. I will not let you down."

Bavarian Alps, February, 1945

The train had been traveling slowly for two days through the white wilderness. Across from Hilbert sat his companion for the journey. Dressed in a black SS uniform with silver skulls on the collar, SS Sturmbannführer, Karl Roth was a veteran of the Russian Front. He spoke infrequently and the scar on his right cheek gave him a very intimidating expression. "We should be there soon," Sommer said.

"Hmm," Roth grunted.

The scenery outside slipped by. The mountain peaks stood out with their giant, gray-faced slabs and white caps. The pines had taken on a silvery look and a low white mist hung in the valleys.

"I will take care of the driver and engineer when we arrive," Roth said curtly making it the first time he'd spoken more than one word in the past fifty miles. "Then we both will take care of the escort."

Sommer nodded. "Alright."

The train passed through another valley; this one had a lake nestled in the bottom of it. During summer, the scene would be stunning. The line followed a steep escarpment around the lake and at the end it approached a solid wall of rock.

On the other side of the lake a man was chopping wood near a cabin. He stopped what he was doing and listened. A train? No, it must be the wind in the trees. He went back to splitting wood. He heard it again. Yes, a train. How could there be a train in this valley; there wasn't even a line. Then he saw it, a line of dark smoke billowing above the pines on the other side of the lake. "Good Lord."

Three hours later, two men approached the cabin. They were dressed in warm, thick, white clothing. One of them knocked on the door. The man answered. "Good evening," Roth said to the man. "Could you spare a little warmth for a couple of weary travelers?"

The man thought for a moment and asked, "Are you from the train?"

Roth glanced at Sommer. "Yes, we're from the train."

Sommer knew what had to be done.

———

Berlin, Germany, Present Day

"It's in Bavaria," Mark said staring at Brooke wide-eyed. "They put it all on a train and moved it into the Bavarian Alps."

"Do you know where?"

"It doesn't say." Mark looked at Sommer. "Did your father say anything about the train to you?"

He shook his head. "No."

"But you knew about it?" Mark asked holding the diary up.

He nodded. "Yes, but I didn't think much of it. I thought it was just a war story like the rest of his tales."

"So, he did talk to you," Brooke said.

"Yes."

"Do you know where in Bavaria?"

"No. He just said it was in a tunnel safely hidden."

"I'll say it's safely hidden," Mark stated. "Everyone who came into contact with it was killed. We have to get back, Brooke. Now."

As they rose to their feet. Brooke said, "Thank you for your help, Herr Sommer."

"My father wasn't a bad person, Miss Reynolds. Not the man I knew. If it will help, please take the diary."

Brooke nodded. "Thank you. I will return it when we are done."

"Do not forget the artwork."

"We will send someone to collect it," Brooke said. "I believe we can trust you."

He held his hands out helplessly. "Where would I go?"

————

Johann Schmidt glanced up from his computer, the look on his face less than impressed when the door to his office flew open interrupting his video call with an art expert in Spain. He thought about castigating Mark for his rudeness but there was something about the young man's countenance that made him hold his tongue. Then Brooke appeared behind him, and he said, "Ramon, I must go, something important has come up. Can we reschedule?"

"That is fine, Johann," Ramon replied.

The Zoom call disconnected, and Schmidt said, "This had better—"

"We've found it!" Mark exclaimed.

Brooke said. "Johann, could you call the team together, please. They're all going to want to hear this."

"I'll do it now. Conference table in five minutes."

"Thank you."

"We found it," Mark said once more with a large grin, feeling suddenly like the little boy who had found his father's holy grail. "We found it, Mister Schmidt."

———

"All right, everyone is here, now tell us the news," Schmidt said.

"The lead on the driver paid off," Brooke said holding up the diary. She slid it across the table to Turow. "Happy birthday, Greg."

"What is in it?" Schmidt asked.

"I never read it," Brooke said. "Our Sherlock Holmes there did. Oh, by the way, you might want to send someone to the address. He has Julian Falat's Widok Krakowa there."

Mark looked at Isabella whose face lit up like a lighthouse on a stormy night. "Really? It is there? It is not a fake?"

"You'd be the be the best judge of that," Mark said with a grin. "But according to the diary, Hilbert Sommer was given that piece of art by Wolff while all of the other treasures were loaded onto a train in Neustrelitz. Including the Amber Room."

The silence around the gathering was electric. All eyes were on Mark's beaming face. He waited.

"Keep going, Mark, you've got us all hooked," Turow said.

"The convoys all went to Neustrelitz. The train was loaded and then it left for the Bavarian Alps with Sommer and another SS major on board. Wolff appointed them both. He promoted Sommer just before they left."

"Do you know the other officer's name?" Molly asked.

"Roth. Karl Roth. According to Sommer he had a scar on his right cheek."

Molly went to work on her laptop.

"Have you ever heard of Roth, Werner?" Brooke asked the historian.

Krause shook his head. "Probably a fake name."

"Where in the Alps, Mark?" Schmidt asked.

"I'm not sure. It's a valley with a lake."

"That could put them anywhere," Turow said.

"They traveled slowly for a couple of days, that must be something."

Turow nodded. "We still need to be able to narrow it down."

Webster said, "I could hook into a satellite and get some aerial pictures. We might be able to pick out an old railroad path somewhere."

"Yes, do that," Schmidt said. "What else do we know?"

Mark said, "They killed the driver, the engineer, and the escort with them after they hid the train. Also, a man who lived alone in a cabin on the other side of the lake, who witnessed the train's presence."

"That might give me something to work with," Turow said. "Having the treasure hidden in Bavaria would have been preplanned. Wolff being close by in Munich."

"Wolff was planning to build a new Reich," Mark said. "But I guess he died before he got the chance."

Schmidt nodded. "I had Mister Webster do some digging into that. He found out that Wolff had developed some kind of illness while he was incarcerated. It was what eventually killed him."

"All that treasure close by and he could do nothing about it," Mark said.

"Such is life," Brooke said.

A brief silence was ended by Schmidt. "Alright, let's go and learn things, people. We're close, I can feel it."

They all stood, and Mark was approached by Isabella. "Mark, would you like to come with me to get the picture?"

He glanced at Brooke who just shrugged noncommittally. He nodded. "Sure, why not?"

Isabella's smile gleamed. "Great. I'll meet you outside in a few minutes."

"You drive?"

She smiled even wider. "Sure. I am a great driver."

Mark nodded. "I'll see you there."

She hurried off and Mark looked once more at Brooke. She moved closer to him and said in a low voice, "Keep an eye on her. Make sure she stays safe. Here."

Brooke passed Mark her Glock and a spare magazine.

"I—"

"Take it, please."

He nodded. "All right."

"Thank you."

"Wait," Mark said in a hushed voice, placing his hand on Isabella's arm. "Something isn't right."

They were walking along the street towards the apartment block when Mark sensed it. Isabella looked at him curiously. "What's wrong?"

He could see the concern in her eyes. He glanced around trying to find anything out of the ordinary. He took the Glock from his pants and held it down at his side. "I'm not sure. Call Brooke and tell her we're in trouble."

Isabella reached into her pocket for her cell. She took it out and hit the speed dial button that would connect her with Brooke. "Don't tell me he's upset you already," she said on the other end.

"Mark says we are in trouble and for you to come."

"What? Put him on, Bella."

She held out the cell. "Brooke wants to talk to you."

Mark took the cell and put it to his ear. "I'm here."

"Tell me what's happening," Brooke said. He could tell she was walking fast by the change in her voice.

"I'm not sure. It's just a feeling. I could be imagining it, but I don't think so. I can usually trust my gut. It's the same feeling I used to get right before my squad used to get hit in Afghanistan."

"Feelings are good. Saved me many times in the sandbox. Look around you and tell me what you see. Four eyes are better than two."

"That's just it. Everything looks the same as it was this morning."

"Nothing is ever the same, Mark. You know that. Concentrate."

He scanned the street, aware that Isabella had suddenly grasped his free hand. He looked at her and smiled to try and reassure. He looked away again and said to Brooke. "It's quiet. Nobody around. Even the vehicles are mostly still the same."

"Tell me about them."

"Not much to tell."

"You said mostly the same. What ones are different?"

"There's two. A blue Mercedes and a black Audi."

"SUVs or cars?"

"Both cars."

"Where are they parked?"

"The Mercedes is outside the apartment block and the Audi is further along. No, it's not right. We're bugging out."

"All right, I'm on my way."

Mark turned, taking Isabella with him. "What is happening, Mark?"

"We need to leave, Bella."

"All right," she said.

Mark heard a motor start. He looked back and saw the Audi pull away from the curb. "Isabella, get behind the car."

"What?"

"Just do it."

"What's going on, Mark?" Brooke asked firmly.

"I think we're in trouble."

"I'll be as quick as I can."

The following events appeared to happen in slow motion. The Audi's window came down on the passenger side and an automatic weapon appeared. Isabella dove behind the vehicle just as the gun opened fire, wrapping her arms over her head.

Bullets punched into the stationary SUV. Windows shattered, spraying the two crouching figures with glass. Isabella let out a scream and Mark brought the Glock up, oblivious to the hailstorm of lead coming his way, as once again the old Mark surfaced.

The tires on the street side of the SUV blew out and the vehicle rocked onto rims with the violent escape of air.

Mark fired a full magazine at the Audi and saw a window disintegrate and holes appear in the rear quarter panel.

As the fusillade continued, the noise of the impacting lead on the SUV sounded like ballpeen hammers pounding it into submission.

But then the gunfire stopped, and the Audi sped away along the street.

Mark dropped out the empty magazine and reloaded,

his chest heaving as adrenaline coursed through his veins.

With tears streaming down her face, Isabella trembled with fear.

"Bella?"

She looked up at him, the fear still evident in her eyes.

"Are you alright?" he asked her.

"Who were they?" she asked shakily.

"I'm not sure."

Isabella stood and buried her face into his shoulder. "You saved my life, Mark. Thank you."

———

The police came, asking all manner of questions. They arrived before Brooke, taking statements from them both. When Brooke did turn up, Mark had just finished his, but Isabella was still relating hers to a young oberwachtmeister, or senior constable.

"Are you alright, Mark?" Brooke asked him, passing over a bottle of water.

When he reached out to take it, she noticed the tremor in his hand and quickly grasped it in her own. "You did good, Mark. You and Isabella are still alive."

Looking into her face, he noticed the concern in her eyes, and suddenly realized that since joining the Foundation, Brooke had been like a sister to him, watching over his every move. "These people need to be stopped, Brooke. Before more people are killed. Next time it could be one of us."

"Yes, they do. But the main thing was to keep Isabella safe, which you did. There's some soldier left in there after all. Come on, let's get you both back to the Foundation."

11

THE ENEMY'S LAIR

Berlin, Germany

"What happened?" Heinrich Wolfsjunge demanded. "Were my orders not clear?"

Anika Meyer nodded. "They were. I have had the problem dealt with before anything can be traced back to you."

"Already?"

"Yes, sir."

"Maybe I did make the right decision placing you in charge."

"You did."

"You sound almost arrogant," Wolfsjunge said.

"You don't pay me to be nice. You pay me to get the job done."

"I do indeed," he allowed. His eyes narrowed. "But please make sure that this doesn't happen again."

"I will see it doesn't." She hesitated before saying, "It would seem that Mister Butler shouldn't be underestimated. From what the ones responsible told me, he's quite capable."

"His record speaks for itself," Wolfsjunge replied. "Perhaps if they read it, they would have thought twice about what they did."

"Yes, sir."

"There was good news from our informant within the Foundation. They have a diary which belonged to Hilbert Sommer. It tells of a train full of treasure which was hidden in a valley in Bavaria."

"Is it the one?" Meyer asked.

Wolfsjunge smiled. "It indicates that the room is aboard like I suspected."

"All we have to do is find it."

"No. The plan remains the same. We will let them find it and lead us to it."

"As you wish, Herr Kommandant."

———

The following day, Molly went in search of Brooke. There was an air of excitement about her when she found her in the gym working out. "Where's Mark?"

"I'm not sure. He might be taking timeout somewhere."

Molly frowned. "What do you mean? What's wrong?"

"I think he's doubting himself. Thinking about quitting."

"What makes you say that?"

"It's just a feeling."

"Oh, no he can't. Did you tell Johann?"

Brooke shook her head. "No. I wanted to give him a chance to work through it himself."

"I actually have something I thought you two might be interested in," Molly said.

"What's that?" asked Brooke, wiping her face with her towel then throwing it across her shoulders as they began walking together from the gymnasium to the locker rooms where Brooke intended to shower.

"Karl Roth."

"He's alive?" Brooke asked hopefully.

"No, he died in nineteen forty-nine."

"Dang it."

"He has a daughter though," Molly said.

"Where?"

"Berlin cemetery."

Brooke sighed. "You're just full of good news, Roberts."

"However, the daughter had a son who is very much alive."

"Great. That's something at least. Where can we find him?"

"His name is Kurt Stuber," Molly told her.

Brooke stopped walking, took a mouthful from her water bottle, and turning to Molly, frowned. "Where have I heard that name before?"

"Stuber Aero Engineering. They make jet engines for different aircraft manufacturers around the globe."

Brooke's jaw dropped. "Good grief, the guy is a multi-millionaire."

"Something like that."

"Now I'm going to have to see if I can get an appointment with him. I'll run it past Johann; he might know of a way. But first I need to hit the shower."

"Good luck," Molly said with a tentative smile. "With the meeting, not the shower."

Brooke sighed. "I have a feeling I'm going to need it."

———

Molly left Brooke to her problems and ablutions and made her way to the breakroom for a water, finding Mark huddled in a corner of one of the sofas. "Hey, Sport. Why so glum?"

"Why do you have pink hair?" Mark asked, looking up at the new arrival.

"I suppose I could tell you that it's what makes me, me," Molly replied getting a bottle of water. "But that wouldn't be true."

"No?"

"No. The real reason was my parents—well my dad and stepmom; actually, it was just my stepmom—didn't like me."

"Your dad didn't like you?"

"He did, but Athena was a real cow."

"So, you went a radical color because of that?"

Molly shrugged. "In a way. She talked my dad into sending me away to a Catholic boarding school. Get this, it was ten miles away from where I lived, but that cow wanted me gone."

"So, what, you colored your hair before you went?"

"No. I did it while I was there. The mother superior just about had a foal. The old hag made me scrub floors until it grew out."

Mark laughed.

"Your father used to laugh too every time I mentioned it."

Mark stopped. "You got on with him?"

Molly nodded. "Sure. If ever I had a problem, I always went to him to talk it over. I don't know why; maybe he was wise, but he was just nice like that, and super easy to talk to."

"I'm glad someone could," Mark said a little woodenly.

"Oh, dear. I'm sorry."

"No, it's all right. Really. Tell me, how did you come to work for Johann?"

"After I was sent to the Catholic school—as you already know—I kind of went off the rails. Mostly because I was angry with my father. While I was there, I became good with computers and had a passion for history. I'm not as good as Webster but I can hold my own. Then Johann came to the school one day with Greg. I guess I'd been hacking into the wrong database. The rest is history."

"What about Oxford?"

"Johann put me through. The old guy is more of a father to me than my own."

"What about your parents? Your dad, anyway?"

"I haven't seen him for years. These guys are more family to me."

Mark nodded.

"I was talking to Brooke. She said she's afraid you were thinking about calling it quits."

"Yeah." Mark looked down, not wanting her to see the doubt on his face.

"Why?"

He hesitated for several moments before admitting slowly, "I'm not sure if I fit. Yesterday scared the crap out of me."

"It would me, too. Getting shot at."

"No, not that. I'm used to being shot at, but it does something to me and it costs lives of those around me."

"What do you mean?"

"It doesn't matter," he said with a shake of his head.

"Well, it didn't, and Isabella says you're her new hero."

"I don't know." He continued looking down, picking at his fingernails while trying to gauge his part in what had happened.

Molly said. "Stick with Brooke. Your father trusted her no end. You should too."

"Except he wound up dead," Mark pointed out.

"Yes, but I think if he knew that he was going to be shot at on that day, he'd still put his life in Brooke's hands. She was shot too; did you know that?"

Mark shook his head. "No, I didn't know."

"Well, now you do. We all want you to stay, Mark. We're starting to get used to you hanging around. And you've proven to be a real asset in our search so far. You've a real knack for it. I think you've found your niche."

Mark hesitated, not quite reassured by her words, but felt not as unsure about his place here. "I'll stay for now."

Molly put down her water bottle and hugged him with a smile. "Good for you. Now, if you find Brooke, she might have something for you to do. I think she'll be in Johann's office."

―――――

Mark knocked lightly on the door and waited for the invitation to enter. When it came, he opened the door and saw Brooke standing to one side. Schmidt watched him enter and close the door behind him. "Hello, Mark, how are you feeling today?"

"I'm fine, thank you, sir."

"That is good. Is there something I can help you with?"

"No, sir. I was just looking for Brooke. Molly told me there was something she might need my help with."

Brooke eyed him cautiously. "I might, but only if you think you're up to it."

"I'll be fine."

"All right. Molly found out that Roth had a daughter. She died but left a son. His name is Kurt Stuber."

Mark frowned. "I have a feeling I should know that name."

"Think multimillionaire who manufactures jet engines."

"The same guy who was investigated three years ago about a crash in Egypt?"

Brooke wracked her brain and then said, "You know you could be right there. Johann?"

The billionaire nodded. "That's him. His defense cost him millions, but he got out of it by the skin of his teeth."

"Sounds like an interesting man," Mark mused.

"Oh, he is," Schmidt said with a wave of his hand, indicating Brooke. "I was just telling Brooke to tread easy with him."

"Do you mind if I come with you?" Mark asked her.

She smiled at him. "Sure. I can use the company. Let's go."

Once they were outside Schmidt's office Brooke stopped and turned to face Mark. "Are you sure you are alright?"

"I'm fine." He gave a weak grin which did nothing to fill her with confidence.

"That's good," she told him but not really believing it herself.

"Why didn't you tell me you were shot, too, the day my father died?" Mark asked suddenly changing the subject away from himself.

Brooke shrugged. "I don't know. Didn't think it was important."

"It was to me," Mark told her. "It makes all the difference."

"In what way?"

"Well, I was ready to leave today. Right up until the moment I found out that you were almost killed with my father."

Brooke just stared at him. Mark continued, his face taking on a determined expression, "I want you to teach me everything you do around here. Don't leave anything out. Get me a weapon, too. If I am going to stay here, I need to be able to look after everyone around me. We'll be a team."

She hesitated momentarily before agreeing. "All right," she said. "I'll teach you all I know."

"Thank you."

"You know, this is one of those moments where your father would be proud of you, don't you?"

"Maybe."

"Since he's not here to do the honors," she said, walking over to him, "I'll do it."

Brooke wrapped her arms around Mark and pulled him close. There was nothing for him to do but return the embrace which he did with gusto.

"Before I do this, Mark, there's something I need to know. If I'm going to trust you, I want to know what you're holding back."

He stepped back and stared into her eyes. "What do you mean?"

"You're hiding something to do with your military record. I want to know what."

"You've read it?"

"Yes, but there's something lying beneath the surface. You had a distinguished, albeit brief, career. Awarded the Silver Star for bravery. Served—"

She stopped when she saw his expression change at the mention of the silver star. She nodded slowly. "What happened?"

There was conflict in his gaze, but he started anyway. "I was on patrol with my squad in Afghanistan. There were reports of insurgents and Taliban in the area. My commanding officer wanted a short patrol to check it out.

He normally would have sent out a platoon, but we were undermanned. So, I drew the short straw. Everything went fine until we were on the homeward leg. That's when the Taliban hit us. Fifty against ten. After they started, I was already two men down. Both were wounded and out in the open. One of my other men, a guy from Roanoke, Gilbert, funny guy, the joker of the squad, went out to try and get them in. He made it three feet before he was hit and killed."

Brooke waited for him to continue.

"I ordered the rest of them to hold their positions and to keep up their fire. All the time while they did it, the wounded guys were calling out for help. My guys kept at me to let them go and get our boys. But I wouldn't let them."

Brooke nodded.

"Eventually the Taliban fighters targeted the two wounded men, teasing us by shooting at them but not hitting them. Eventually it became too much and a young private threw his weapon down and was about to go out when I managed to stop him."

"What about the rest of your people back at the FOB?" Brooke asked.

"We couldn't reach them. Our radio was screwed up."

"What happened next?"

"I went out and got them myself," Mark replied. "I wasn't about to let my guys do something I wasn't prepared to do myself. So, out I went."

"And you got them both?"

"Yes, ma'am. Not that it did any good. They both died an hour later while we were still pinned down because I couldn't get a medevac in to get them out."

"Not your fault."

"I was their senior NCO. It rests on me."

"How did you get them out?"

"We slipped out after dark. Took the dead with us."

"And they gave you the silver star."

"Yeah, for getting my men killed."

"Not your fault, remember that."

"You know, this is the first time I've really talked about it."

Brooke nodded. "Thank you."

Mark shrugged. "Maybe I needed it."

"Maybe."

———

Kurt Stuber was in his late forties with hair so blond it was almost platinum. His office took up most of the top floor of a forty-four-floor office complex which had been opened the previous year, and he now sat behind a large wooden desk, looking up at the pair standing in front of him. Mark wrinkled his nose at the new smell which still permeated the building.

After they had introduced themselves, Stuber gave them both a broad smile as he stood and directed them towards three leather chairs situated near one of the large glass panels with a commanding view of the city. "Please, have a seat. Would you like some refreshments?"

"Thank you, but no," Brooke said politely.

"What about you, Mark, was it?" Stuber asked.

"Yes, it is, and no, thank you."

Stuber rubbed his hands together. "Fine, fine. How can I be of help to you?"

"We'd like to ask you a couple of questions about your grandfather if that's all right?" Brooke started.

A puzzled look on his face, he said, "Of course. I'm not sure how much I can help though. I barely knew the man."

"After he passed, was there anything handed down to the family?"

"Like?"

"A diary, or something along those lines, from his time in the war?"

Stuber shook his head. "No, nothing like that. Why do you ask?"

Mark said, "The Schmidt Foundation has linked your grandfather and another man to a Nazi treasure train loaded with many artifacts towards the end of the war."

"Really? That's interesting," Stuber said. "Can you tell me more? I'd be interested to hear all about it."

"He and another man were appointed personally to escort the train to its destination."

"Where?"

"I—"

"We can't say at this point in time," Brooke interrupted, cutting Mark off before he could say too much.

Stuber nodded. "I understand. What was this other man's name? Maybe I might have heard it before."

"It was Hilbert Sommer."

Stuber looked thoughtful for a moment before shaking his head. "No, I don't think so."

"That's all right," Brooke said. "It was worth a shot."

Mark said, "You have some nice paintings on the walls of your office, Mister Stuber."

"Yes, they are, aren't they? I've picked up a few pieces over the years. Do you like art?"

Mark shrugged. "It's all right, I guess. But I'm no expert."

Stuber chuckled. "I'm not either. I just like the look of them."

With a smile, Mark said, "May I look at them while you discuss things with Brooke?"

"Why not? Be my guest."

Mark walked over to the paintings and looked at them one by one. Behind him he heard Brooke ask, "Mister Stuber, have you ever heard of the name Gerhard Wolff?"

"No, I don't think so."

He continued to talk but by that time Mark had slipped out of earshot.

Mark stopped. Standing near the wall was a glass cube sitting atop a pedestal. He stared at the contents, his head starting to spin. Inside on display were three gold watches. If Mark had to guess he figured they would be worth a fortune. He glanced back at Brooke and Stuber. They were still talking.

Mark flicked through the stored files in his head trying to remember where he'd seen the items before. Then he remembered and had to bite his tongue to keep from calling out. This was a different man he was dealing with here. The man was loaded with money and lawyers as well.

Mark drew himself away from the watches and along to the next painting. From behind him, Brooke called out, "Are you ready to go, Mark?"

He turned and nodded.

Stuber asked, "Did you like what you saw?"

"I guess so," Mark replied. "Although I think a couple of them could use a few art lessons."

Stuber laughed out loud. "I might have to agree with you."

They said their goodbyes and thanked Stuber for his time before heading along the hallway to the elevator. Brooke glanced at Mark and said, "What has you all wound up?"

"You can tell, huh? I'll fill you in once we get outside."

They rode the elevator to the ground floor and hurried through the foyer and outside to where their SUV was parked. Once in the privacy of the vehicle, Brooke turned to Mark and said, "Spill. I know it's something big. Your father used to get the same expression on his face when he was excited."

Mark told her.

Stuber sat by himself after they left and waited patiently until Anika entered the office. He looked at her and said, "Well?"

"He seemed taken with the watches," she informed him.

"I was afraid of that," Stuber replied. "I'll have them put away before Interpol comes to visit. Along with the paintings."

"If you don't mind me saying so, sir, he is becoming more trouble than he is worth."

"What do you propose we do about it?"

"Take him, bring him back here to work for us."

Stuber considered the proposal for a while before nodding. "Fine. Do it."

"Are you sure?" Schmidt asked.

"Yes, sir. I'm certain of it. My father had all kinds of books lying around the house. I'd flick through them, and these three watches were definitely in one."

"After all these years. You're totally sure?"

"Yes, sir. The gold watches of King Augustus II, King Stanisław Leszczyński, and Queen Marie Casimire."

"We'll need to notify the correct authorities—"

"I'd hold off on that, Johann," Brooke said. "There's something off about this guy."

"I agree," Mark said. "He made out like he knew nothing about art and such, but he knew more than what he was letting on."

"You think they were acquired illegally?" Schmidt asked. "I know the watches would have been, but what about the paintings?"

"I'm sure I've seen some of them before."

"Get together with Isabella. See if you can come up with a list."

"Yes, sir."

"If what you say is true, this could be a tremendous find."

"I agree, sir."

"I'm starting to think having you here was a good move, Mister Butler. A good move indeed."

"I'll go and find Isabella now," Mark said.

Once he was gone, Brooke said to the billionaire, "Mark asked me to bring him up to speed with everything I do."

"I see. And are you?" Schmidt asked, leaning forward with interest.

"I think it would be best," Brooke said. "But I wanted to make sure you were on board with it before we started."

Schmidt nodded. "Fine. It can't hurt. When will you start?"

"I was thinking of doing some this afternoon. Take him out to the range where the Spezialeinsatzkommando train; run through their course with him on my shoulder. Get a gauge on what his combat skills are like."

"Train him. If he gets into trouble through no fault of his own, then I can work it out. But warn him that if he does anything stupid, I will leave him to suffer the consequences."

"I'll train him right, Johann. Have no doubt."

"That's them," Mark said to Isabella as they stared at the computer screen. "That's the last one."

Isabella nodded with satisfaction. "All three by Canaletto. This is quite a find. They were taken from the National Museum of Warsaw. Most everything that was there was destroyed by German soldiers. However, some were thought to have survived. Obviously, some did. We won't know until we get to look at them. I'll have to let Johann know. He'll get Interpol involved and they will go in and rescue them. We'll have to be careful; Stuber is like butter."

Mark gave her a curious look. "Butter?"

"Nothing gets stuck to him."

"Teflon," Mark corrected her. "The saying is Teflon."

Isabella looked embarrassed. "I'm sorry."

Mark touched her arm. "Don't apologize."

Isabella regained her composure and smiled, touching his hand with hers. "Mark, will you eat with me tonight?"

Mark hesitated a moment then said, "Sure, we both have to eat right?"

"Good. I will talk to you later about where we should go."

"Am I interrupting anything?" Brooke asked.

They turned in their chairs to face her. Isabella said, "No. We were talking about a—a date. Is that what it is called?"

"Good grief," Brooke muttered.

Mark gave Brooke a sideways look before saying slowly, "Bella asked me to eat with her tonight. That's all."

Isabella's face turned red. "I must go and see Johann. This is too good to let go."

She came out of her seat, quickly gathered her notes, and hurried off.

"You're with me. Let's go."

"Where are we going?"

"A little field trip."

12

THE KIDNAPPING

"The Special Shooter Police guys train here?" Mark said because he kept butchering the correct pronunciation of the name.

"Spezialeinsatzkommando," Brooke said.

The place was huge. The complex itself covered ten acres of close-quarters combat training with both indoor and outdoor courses. Brooke pointed to a large warehouse. "We'll be going in there. We just need to get equipped."

"I see you have brought a lamb to the slaughter, Brooke," a booming voice said from behind them.

They turned and Mark's jaw dropped. Standing before them was the biggest anything Mark had ever seen before. Bigger than any of the guys he'd served with. Brooke said, "Hello, Felix."

Felix pointed at Mark. "Who is this warrior?"

"His name is Mark. He's Frank's son."

Felix nodded somberly. He stepped forward and put out his right hand. "Pleased to meet you, Mark. I was sorry to hear about your father."

Mark considered himself reasonably tall, but this man

mountain stood head and shoulders above him. When they shook, Mark's hand was engulfed by Felix's. "Good to meet you too, er, sir."

The giant smiled. "You will call me Felix."

Mark nodded.

"Felix is the commander of one of the special reaction squads that train here. They're like special forces for special forces."

"Like SEAL Team Six," Mark said.

"Sort of, yes." Brooke looked at Felix. "Where is everyone?"

"They are doing other things," he said and left it at that. "I believe you are here for a reason?"

Brooke told him and he nodded. "Indoor or outdoor course?"

"Indoor."

"Come with me and I'll get you set up."

Thirty minutes later, the pair were wearing harnesses, and Brooke was armed with a Heckler and Koch 45 Tactical handgun.

"Does that thing fire real bullets?" Mark asked.

Felix chuckled. "No. Only blanks. The practice range is rigged for electronic only today. This is why you wear the special harnesses. When the targets appear, they will either be good or bad. If you shoot the wrong one an electric pulse will flow through the harness and give a shock to the wearer. Nothing too bad. Only a little jolt. The same will happen if you take too long in identifying and suppressing a bad target."

Brooke said, "You will come with me on the first run through. You'll stay on my shoulder and go nowhere. Understood? Felix will watch from the control room."

Mark thought back to basic training, but said, "Okay."

Felix said, "I'll get the course ready. You go to the first

door." He reached out and opened a large hand in front of Mark. "Take these. You'll need them."

A small packet containing a set of earplugs was dwarfed by the meaty palm.

Mark took the packet, tore it open, and put them in. He followed Brooke as she moved along a narrow passage to the first door. She turned to Mark. "Are you ready?"

"Yep."

"Put your left hand on my right shoulder and don't remove it."

He extended his hand and did as he was ordered. Brooke said loudly, "Whenever you're ready, Felix."

The big man's voice boomed over the loudspeaker. "Go."

Brooke reached out and opened the door before passing through it. Her handgun was up and sweeping the first room. Mark had hold of her shoulder and followed her at arm's length. The room was dressed as a living room and at first glance it seemed empty. Then suddenly a target appeared, pointing a gun at them.

The weapon in Brooke's hand barked twice immediately, the noise even through his earplugs making Mark jump. The target disappeared. She walked towards another door and opened it. Beyond the obstruction was a hallway. She started along it, weapon raised. Another target appeared but Brooke held her fire. This target was a young girl and no threat.

The target disappeared and almost immediately another appeared. The gun barked twice more, and the target slid back into the wall.

Halfway along the hallway on the left was another room. Brooke swung into it and swept her weapon left to right as she walked around inside. This one was made up into a bedroom.

No targets appeared.

The next thing Mark knew they were out into the hallway again.

Brooke paused at the end of the hallway before she paused. Something, some kind of sixth sense warned her, and she said, "Against the wall."

Without question, Mark followed her lead and pressed up against the wall. Suddenly it sounded as though someone was hitting the door with a hammer. "What's that?" Mark shouted.

"It simulates someone shooting at the door," Brooke called out.

A voice said over the loudspeaker, "Well done, Brooke. You still have those wonderful instincts."

Brooke ignored the compliment and opened the door. The gun in her hand barked again and a target holding some kind of automatic weapon slid onto the floor. She swept the rest of the room set up as a kitchen. No more targets.

They passed through the kitchen and out another door. This time the landscape changed. A large open plan office stood before them; small cubicles formed by a maze of partitions held any number of individuals working at their desks.

A target stood up. A man wearing a suit. Brooke held her fire and moved to her right, Mark in tow. The target lowered and another took its place. This one was of a terrorist holding a worker hostage. Brooke pivoted and fired without any hesitation.

"The Frau has skills," Felix's voice boomed again.

From the office, Brooke and Mark worked their way through four more rooms. Another office, a café, a restaurant, and a nightclub which was darkened. Along the way Brooke stopped to reload once.

By the time they reached the far end Felix was waiting

for them. He nodded with appreciation. "You never fail to impress me, Brooke."

"I'm a little rusty."

"Ha," he exploded and looked at Mark. "Rusty, she says. I know men in this unit who could not hold a candle to her skills."

Brooke turned to Mark. "Your turn."

"All right." He smiled.

"Yes, it's time to see how you go through the course."

"Cool. Let's see what I remember."

"You will be fine," Felix said. "I will turn the shock off so that it will not zap you."

"Well, all right."

Brooke gave him the weapon and a couple of magazines. "Go to the start line."

Mark went back to the doorway where it all started and waited for the fun to begin.

———

Brooke and Felix stood in the control room and watched Mark as he worked his way through the course. Every now and then they'd glance at each other and nod or wince depending on what had happened. All the while they could see him getting more and more frustrated. By the time Mark had emptied the spare magazine he still had one room to go.

What happened next surprised them both. Felix brought a target into play and Mark raised the weapon to fire. When it remained silent Felix said, "He's empty."

While they watched, Mark dropped the weapon and ran at the target, launching himself at it and hitting it hard with his shoulder. The target was a lot solider than Mark figured and he came off second best. Felix said, "That's different."

"Shows initiative," Brooke said.

"Let's get down there before he gets hurt or breaks something."

When they reached Mark, they found him still in a frustrated state. When he saw them walk up, the words that tumbled from his mouth were, "I want to try it again."

"Take it easy, Rambo," Brooke told him. "We'll be back. You won't get it perfect overnight. You're a bit rusty, that's all."

Felix said, "My friend, the next time you return, we will put you on the outdoor course."

Mark nodded. "All right. Thanks."

"In the meantime, take this."

Felix produced a baseball cap from behind his back with a bold SEK on it. Mark asked, "What's SEK?"

"Spezialeinsatzkommando," Felix said with pride.

"Thank you," Mark said with a grin.

"Before you go," Felix spoke. "Maybe we could put him on the indoor range to see if he can hit a target, yes?"

Brooke nodded. "What do you say, Mark?"

"Sure."

Chatting to Brooke the whole way, Felix escorted them to another part of the complex. It looked like another big warehouse and when they entered, Felix set him up with a Glock. He ran out a paper target and said to Mark. "Whenever you are ready, my friend."

Mark fired nine shots and placed the weapon on the bench in front of himself. The target whirred in and they all looked at it in awe. Felix was the first to speak. "I've never seen that before."

"It's certainly remarkable," Brooke replied.

"I didn't even hit it," Mark said astounded.

"I'm confused," Brooke said. "At the Foundation's range you handled it expertly. Misspent youth and military were your exact words."

"Didn't you check it?" Mark asked.

"Yes, they were all in the center of the torso."

Felix grinned. He took out a magazine from his pocket and gave it to Mark. "Here, try this one."

Brooke's lips thinned. "You're a monster, Felix. You gave him a magazine of blanks, didn't you?"

"Maybe."

Mark shook his head as her reloaded the handgun. Felix reset the target and said, "Try again, my friend."

Mark raised the Glock once more and fired off the full magazine without stopping. This time when the target came back it had two areas where the rounds had struck. Center mass and the head. Felix nodded. "He can shoot."

Brooke smiled. "Yes, he can."

———

"What did Johann do about Kurt Stuber?" Brooke asked Turow.

"He had a long discussion with the head of Interpol and that's all I know."

"Maybe they'll keep tabs on him."

"I doubt it. No one wants to touch him. They're scared something will come down from above and end their careers."

Brooke looked at her watch. It was four in the afternoon. Just enough time to drag Mark across the mats. "I'll catch up with you later," she said to Turow.

She walked over to Mark and said, "Come on, you. Let's go."

He looked up at her. "Where?"

"The gym. We'll go and practice some hand-to-hand defensive stuff."

He climbed to his feet. Mark walked over to the refrigerator and opened the door. He looked inside and then closed it, shaking his head.

Brooke frowned. "What's wrong?"

"I was looking to see if there was a salami in there, I thought maybe I could use it to beat you with."

She smiled. "Smarty pants. Come on."

"I think I saw a banana in there," he replied. "Or maybe it was a head of lettuce."

"Move it."

———

The place Isabella chose for them to eat wasn't far from the Foundation, but Mark had to admit, it was nice. Framed pictures of Italy hung on every wall. From Rome to Venice, and even Milan. The place was rich with the scent of cooking food.

It served pizza the likes he'd never eaten before. Isabella smiled at him when he'd finished the last piece of their second pie. "I was beginning to think you didn't like it."

"It was okay," he said with a smile.

"Shall we go back to the Foundation now then?"

"Sure."

He got up from his seat and walked around to help Isabella up from hers. She said, "Grazie caro amico." *Thank you, dear friend.*

After paying the check, the pair wandered outside into the cool but pleasant evening. They started along the sidewalk with intermittently spaced plantings of tall trees along its length. Streetlights were strategically placed to provide the best illumination. Isabella hooked her handbag over her shoulder and hugged herself as though cold.

A car drove past them on the street and Mark found himself subconsciously checking it out. Blue Audi, tinted windows, plate number—

"Did you hear what I said?" Isabella stopped walking before asking.

"I'm sorry?"

"What's wrong?

He looked up and saw the same blue Audi, the same tinted windows, and the same plate. This time it slowed. Isabella saw Mark's body stiffen and he pulled away. She drew her head back and stared at his face. But instead of posing a question, she looked to where his gaze was fixed. She too saw the Audi driving slowly.

But then brake lights shone red in the night, the car coming to a stop. Just sat there. Mark expected it to reverse toward them, but it never moved. He eased Isabella away from him and said, "Go back to the Foundation, quickly."

"Mark?"

"I think they're after me. You go. Run. Don't stop."

She turned and began to run. Not looking back as Mark had told her. There was a screech of tires and the Audi spun around and drove back towards Mark. As he stood there waiting on the sidewalk, he took out his cell phone, kicking himself that he'd left his newly authorized weapon back at the foundation. Hitting the speed dial a connection was made, he said, "They've come for me."

Without ending the call, he tucked the phone into his shorts, hoping that they wouldn't search for it there.

The Audi's tires chattered on the asphalt as it came to a halt and two people wearing hoods leaped out. Mark remained still, waiting for the inevitable. Within moments, they'd slipped a black bag over Mark's head and bundled him roughly into the car.

They did it without speaking and Mark let them do it. They didn't even check him for the cell. They didn't need to. It had fallen out with all the jostling.

13

THE WOLF'S HIDEOUT

When Brooke arrived on the scene Mark was long gone. She did, however, find his cell still on the pavement. Looking about in desperation, she saw no further trace or clue. Isabella had told her about the blue Audi and that Mark had told her to run. The girl was shattered at having left Mark behind to whatever fate was in store for him. Leaving Isabella at the Foundation with Molly taking care of her, Brooke had set off.

Now at the scene, she reached into her pocket and took out her cell. Punching in a number, she continued to look around while waiting for an answer. When it came, she said, "What have you got?"

Webster said, "Two men took him and bundled him into a blue Audi. From there they took off along the street and disappeared."

"Disappeared to where?"

"I'm not sure. I'm still trying to find them."

"Try harder. Could you get any kind of an ID on them?"

"Not yet. They had hoods on and the number on the car came back as it being stolen."

"All right, keep on it. Let me know when you have something."

"Yes, ma'am."

Brooke disconnected and dialed another number. As soon as the call was answered she said, "I need your help."

"Where are you?"

"Weidenstraße."

"I'll be there shortly."

"Thanks."

———

After pacing the pavement for ten minutes, she looked up as Felix, the big Spezialeinsatzkommando, arrived in an equally big Humvee. He climbed out and looked at Brooke. "What is the problem?"

"Mark has been kidnapped."

Felix's face grew stern. "I see. Did you call it in?"

"I called you."

He nodded. "What do you know?"

Brooke filled him in on the few details that she knew. "He called me just before they took him, to let me know what was happening."

"Do you have any idea who might be behind it?" Felix asked.

Brooke hesitated.

"Brooke?"

"It could be—I'm not sure—but maybe—"

"Brooke?"

"Kurt Stuber."

A pained expression came over his face. "*Gute Trauer.*" *Good grief.*

"I know, but his name came up in our investigation and we needed to question him. We found artifacts there that he shouldn't have had."

Felix said, "All right, but tell me why your friend?"

"He's been making progress. Much more progress than his father ever did."

"Progress of what?"

"We've been tracking a treasure. Some of which came from Carinhall. Some from Königsberg Castle."

"The Amber Room?"

"Yes," Brooke replied. "According to records there were three convoys, each with different destinations. None of them made it. We tracked them to a train which disappeared in the Bavarian Alps. Short version, someone with the treasure train tracks back to Stuber."

"So, you went and talked to him?"

"Yes."

"Why then would he take your friend?"

A car sped past along the street, making her wait to answer. "Maybe he wants the treasure for himself. Maybe he figures he has some kind of right to it."

"So he could have kidnapped him to make him help?"

"Yes, possibly."

"All right then, give me a minute."

Brooke waited as Felix made a call. As he placed his phone back in his pocket, he said, "I've got some people keeping an eye on Stuber. If Mark shows up there, they will see him. There is always the possibility that they won't take him to Stuber."

"I know that."

"All right, then. Let's see if we can find him."

The Audi drove for at least two hours before slowing to a stop. All that time Mark was wearing the hood and his captors remained silent. When the car finally came to a standstill, he heard the doors open and felt the Audi rock as those within alighted.

Hands grasped him roughly and pulled him from the back seat. He heard boots crunch on gravel and could smell the scent of pines as he was pushed away from the car. The gravel ended and he soon found himself on firmer footing. Then came the steps. His foot caught and he almost fell, held upright by the strong grips of his captors. He took a deep breath and continued blindly.

The light changed inside of wherever they were. Footsteps echoed on the hard floor, and he guessed the ceiling was high.

A few minutes later, he was seated on a chair and his arms tied down. The hood came off and Mark blinked, trying to adjust his eyes to the sudden light. He glanced around taking note of everything he could see. He was in a large hall. The walls looked to be built from stone. One of the hooded men brought a small table and placed it in front of Mark. Then came a laptop which he opened before tapping a few keys.

It wasn't long before a picture appeared on the screen. It was a man who, like Mark's captors, wore a hood. But what really drew his attention was the watermark down in the bottom right of the screen. It was a Parteiadler.

"Good evening, Mister Butler." The voice was heavily accented.

Mark remained silent.

"My name is Heinrich Wolfsjunge. I am the leader of The New Nazi Party."

Mark continued his silence.

"Nothing to say?" Wolfsjunge asked.

"Why am I here?"

"Why indeed," the hooded man said. "I wish to make you an offer."

"What kind of offer?" Mark asked.

"I wish you to come and work for us," Wolfsjunge said.

Mark opened his mouth to speak but the hooded figure cut him off. "Think very carefully about how you answer, Mister Butler."

"What if I don't want to?" Mark asked. "Your men take me home?"

"I do not think so."

"So, what you're saying is that if I don't help you, the ones who killed my father, I could suffer the same fate?"

"In a manner of speaking."

Mark thought for a moment. The longer he stayed alive, the more chance the Foundation had of finding him. "I don't see that I have much choice."

"I knew you would see sense."

"What now?" Mark asked.

"My people will give you some of the information that we have so you can look over it. Although I don't know if it will be necessary because you possibly know more than we do."

A folder was placed in front of Mark and his arms untied so he could flick through the package of data he was being supplied with. Most of what was there, the Foundation already knew. The convoys, the diversions, and the loading onto the train. Even the valley. He stopped and frowned. They knew virtually everything about the treasure that the Foundation did. Then it occurred to him that someone from inside the Foundation was giving them information. If they wanted him to help them find it, even when they had all the information before him, then there had to be.

He looked up. "You have someone inside the Foundation."

"Why do you say that?" Wolfsjunge asked.

There was no denial, so Mark assumed his guess was spot on. "Who is it?"

"You do not need to know. You should concentrate on the task at hand."

Mark went back to the folder and found what seemed to be a list. Four pages of it. As he started to look through it, he saw that it was a list of everything supposedly on the train. "Where did you get this list?"

"You are not the only resourceful person, Mister Butler."

"Admit it, you suck or you wouldn't be asking me for help," Mark shot back at him.

"Touché."

He kept reading until he came to it. The holy grail of lost treasures. He looked at the masked man. "So, the room was on the train."

"That is what it says on the list."

"How?"

"How what?"

"How do you know it was on the train?"

"I just do."

Mark's heart beat faster. His breathing quickened and the masked man noticed it. "I see the thought of the room excites you."

"It would excite anyone."

"I suppose you're right there. Now, where do you propose that the train is?"

"I don't know?"

"You don't know?"

"Not yet. If I knew where it was, don't you think that your spy would have told you already?"

Ignoring the jibe, Wolfsjunge asked, "What do you need?"

"Maps."

"Of the Alps?"

"Germany, the Alps, I just need maps."

"Then maps are what you shall have."

―――――

"Do your people have anything?" Brooke asked Felix.

"We have a couple of sightings of a blue Audi but nothing concrete just yet," he replied.

"Where were they?" she asked.

Felix grabbed a map and opened it. "We have one here, another here, and this one here."

Brooke looked at the map. Two in the city and one on the outskirts. "What is out here?" she asked pointing at the third place on the map which Felix had indicated.

"Not a lot."

She studied the map further and widened her search. Then her eyes stopped, and her finger stabbed at the map. "There. What's that?"

"Wolfsversteck, or Wolf's Hideout for the uneducated," Felix told her. "It used to be called Falkenschloss but it was changed a few years back."

"Do we know who owns it?"

Felix shrugged. "I can find out."

Brooke looked at her watch. It was past midnight and Mark had been gone for hours. He could be anywhere by now, but she had a feeling about the castle. She waited for Felix to finish his call. Even though she spoke German his words were sometimes hard to pick up. When he was finished, he rejoined her.

"You're going to like this," he said. "The castle's registered owner is a corporation called, wait for it, Gray Wolf Enterprises."

"Gray Wolf?"

"Yes."

"And who owns Gray Wolf Enterprises?" Brooke asked.

"Kurt Stuber."

"That's it!" she exclaimed. "The third Audi has to be the one. They're taking him to the castle."

"You realize that if we get this wrong, we're in a whole heap of trouble."

"Can't you set up your team for recon first?"

Felix nodded. "I can, but—"

"Then do it. Please, Felix. I lost his father; I'll not lose him too."

"I'll see what I can do."

———

For three hours, Mark studied the maps. He traced every rail line that had been in use throughout the Second World War. By then, he'd nailed it down to two. And only one had a lake. "That has to be it," he muttered to himself. His powers of deduction had led him to this one valley; it had to be the one the treasure-filled train had been hidden in.

He looked over at the guard standing against the stone wall. He said, "Tell your boss, I think I know which valley it is."

A few minutes later, Wolfsjunge was back on the computer link. The mask was ever present, but he seemed a little more excited than the last time they'd spoken. "I hear that you have found it?"

"I think so. The valley is called Würger See after the lake."

Wolfsjunge seemed to be preoccupied with something for a moment before he turned his attention back to Mark. "There are no railway lines in that valley."

While the hooded man had been preoccupied, he'd

moved; only marginally but enough for Mark to notice something behind him. It had taken a moment for him to figure out what it was he was seeing but when he did, it all fell into place. He knew exactly who the hooded man was.

"Did you hear me?" Wolfsjunge demanded. "I said there are no rail lines in that valley."

"Not now," Mark replied. "But you forget that this happened at the end of the Second World War. The Germans had constructed many things over the years. Including rail lines. Whether you have discounted that location because of a lack of railway lines now doesn't mean that there hasn't been in the past."

"How certain are you?"

"I'm not, but it's the best insight I can offer at this time. If it's not there, then we start over again."

Wolfsjunge went silent for a time as though deep in thought behind the hood he wore. He nodded slowly and said, "My people will take you to the valley. If you are right, then that is good. If you are wrong—I hope you can swim, Mister Butler."

The team of Spezialeinsatzkommando infiltrated the castle grounds using the lush gardens for cover. There were no roving security patrols which meant no dogs. No dogs was good. Brooke was now dressed in an armored vest, ballistic helmet, and carried a Heckler and Koch G36 with all the modifications including a laser sight to complement the night vision goggles she wore.

She and Felix set up, their position giving them a clear line of sight to the main entrance of the castle. The gravel turnaround at the base of the steps was empty and it gave

Brooke reason for concern. She said, "They're either not here, or have been and gone."

Felix spoke into his comms mic. "Red Team, move towards the main entrance. Blue Team watch the rear. Yellow Team, remain in position."

Each team leader acknowledged the order. As Brooke watched on, five figures emerged from the shadows and approached the castle. They were bent low and had their weapons raised in case of trouble. When they reached a low-cut hedge, they stopped and waited for further orders. Felix held them there no longer than a minute before ordering them in.

"Red Team, breach."

The men leaped over the hedge and ran across the turnaround and up the stairs to the large door barring their way. Two men took up position on each side while the fifth quickly set a breaching charge on the door. Within seconds he was done and backed away from the door. Moments later the charge blew and the team of Kommandos entered the castle.

Felix pressed the transmit button on his radio once more. "Yellow team, follow Red. Blue Team, hold position."

Once more, Kommandos materialized out of the darkness as had the ones before. Felix turned to Brooke. "Come on, let's have a look."

They rose from their hiding position and moved towards the castle.

14

THE TUNNEL

There was no one there. The whole castle was devoid of life; however, evidence of recent habitation and activity was everywhere. The maps and computers were there, so was the chair and the bindings which until lately had secured Mark. Brooke looked at the maps and tried to decipher what they meant.

"All the rooms are clear," Felix informed her. "There is no sign of anyone left here."

"They were though, and not that long ago," Brooke replied.

Felix looked at the maps on the table. "The Alps."

"Yes. I'm assuming they're trying to get Mark to help them find the train," she explained. "I'm guessing he must have found something otherwise they would still be here."

"All right," said Felix. "If he found something, where would it be?"

Brooke shrugged. "Grab a map."

They looked them over until Brooke was almost certain they were barking up the wrong tree. However, she kept coming back to one map in particular. It seemingly looked like all the rest but wasn't. It had a crease in it.

It wasn't as though the map had been folded neatly. It was just one crease down towards one corner of the map. It wasn't even in perspective with the rest of it.

"I hate it when people fold paper maps," Felix said as he saw her frowning at it.

"Me too," Brooke replied. "There's nothing worse than—" She stopped. "It's a message."

"What?" the big Kommando asked.

"It's a message from Mark. He knows I hate paper maps being folded. He's trying to tell us something."

Brooke began studying the map more intently. Especially the folded part. After five minutes of scrutinizing the section she said, "It can't be in here because there are no lakes."

"Don't give up, now," Felix said frowning. "The message is there somewhere."

Then for no apparent reason, Brooke folded the corner of the map up until it lay flat against the rest of it, its tip pointing at a valley in the Alps, the lake that was nestled there giving it its name. She smiled. "Well, I'll be."

Felix nodded. "He is a smart guy."

———

Würger See Valley, Bavarian Alps

The Airbus ACH160 helicopter flew low through the valley, granite-faced peaks on either side. The pilot handled the machine like it was an extension of himself and as they flew, they became one. Mark looked out the window and saw the lake coming up to their right. He could have seen more if he'd been allowed to sit near the window but the two gorillas accompanying him wouldn't hear of it. Across from him were a man and a woman. She was tall, dark-haired, and quite obviously in charge. She caught Mark staring at her and smiled deviously at him.

Shifting his gaze back out the window, Mark noticed the helicopter start to drop lower and slow as it did. The woman opposite him touched her headphones as though listening to a message coming through. Pointing to the headset beside Mark, she indicated for him to put it on. He reached down to picked it up and placed it on his head.

"Look out the window," she ordered him.

He gave her a how am I supposed to do that look.

She tapped the man beside her on the arm and leaned close to him. After a few words, the man rose from his seat and he and Mark swapped places.

This was the first time he'd been close to the woman. She was dressed in black jeans and blouse, her person reeked of some cloying fragrance which he was sure would have been better off left in the shop she'd bought it from. Leaning in close to him, she said, "Look out the window."

Mark turned away from her and gazed down on the lush greenery. Below he could see the lake and large expanses of tall pines. At first, there was nothing glaringly obvious but the longer he stared down, things swam into clarity for him. It seemed to snake along the side of the lake, overgrown by tall grass but it was there. An old rail line bed. Who knew if the tracks were still there, but this was the break they needed. He turned his head to the woman. "That's it. Take us down."

———

The group of five walked along the old rail line. The ties, ballast and rails were still there, hidden beneath the thick vegetation. Mark was surprised by the discovery when they'd walked up the rail bank and found them there. Before touching down, the woman had made a call.

Now they were following the line further along past the lake, the hills surrounding them covered by pines and granite cliffs.

"How much further?" the woman asked.

Mark looked at her. "How should I know that? Do you know how far this rail line goes? I'm not a fortune teller."

"Don't get smart with me. Keep walking."

They continued at a steady pace for another thirty minutes before Mark heard something and he turned to look back the way they'd come. He could see nothing beyond the bend in the line but there was something back there. He was sure of it.

"Get off the track," the woman ordered brusquely.

Mark followed the group off the side, curious to know what was happening. About a minute later, the source of the noise came into view. An orange diesel locomotive was coming towards them. Mark glanced at the woman questioningly. "We will need a train to get the treasure out of there."

It stopped beside them, and they all clambered on board the external platform. The locomotive lurched forward and continued pushing through the grass and vegetation growing amongst the ties and rails.

Ten minutes later, the locomotive came to an abrupt halt, as any further progress was blocked by a large rock-slide swallowing the tracks. "This has to be it," Mark said. "Beyond that slide somewhere is what we're looking for."

The woman picked two men and pointing to the rise beyond the slide, said, "Up there, see what you can find."

The men commenced the climb, finding it difficult to walk upright, traversing the steep terrain making their progress slow. Mark looked at the woman and asked, "What's your name?"

"I am Anika Meyer."

"No relation to Panzer Meyer?" Mark asked jokingly.

Kurt 'Panzer' Meyer was a staunch Nazi who had been tried for war crimes, accused of ordering the death of unarmed allied prisoners in the German town of Aurich. He'd been found guilty and sentenced to death. The sentence was later commuted to life in prison. However, he was released from prison on 7 September 1954.

Anika's face remained deadpan. "He was my great grandfather."

"Remind me that jokes and you don't mix."

A whistle pierced the clear mountain air and they looked up. Standing atop a low ridge above them was one of the men that Anika had sent up there. He was waving for them to follow.

Up the steep and rocky slope, they climbed slowly until reaching the top where they stopped and looked down to where the rear side fell away somewhat. The man said, "There is an opening down further. Most likely an air vent shaft."

"Show me," Anika said curtly.

They made their way down the back face of the hill to a flat area where they found the vent. It was only wide enough to accommodate one person at a time and when Anika looked inside the shaft, she could see rungs welded to the side of it. "Did Hans go down?"

The man nodded. "Yes."

Anika reached into the pack she was carrying and

retrieved a small flashlight. She switched it on to make sure it worked before placing it in her pocket and starting her descent.

———

Anika was surprised to see that when she emerged from the vent, she was able to step down onto the top of a box car. Hans was waiting for her and couldn't hide his enthusiasm. "We have found it."

"We will wait for the others and then look around."

Mark emerged from the vent next and was as surprised as the rest of them to find that he was atop the treasure train. Anika said, "You were right after all."

"This is unbelievable," Mark stated.

The tunnel smelled musty, the air seemingly old. Once the others had joined them, they climbed from the box car and found themselves standing amongst the bones of the dead. Mark winced as he stood on a leg bone, and it cracked crisply under his weight. He muttered a quick sorry under his breath, taking in the magnitude of people who had died down here as Anika swung her small flashlight around. The bones were scattered everywhere. Mark frowned as he said, "There's too many."

"What?" Anika asked.

"I said there are too many. From the diary I read there weren't this many guarding the train."

"Then what do you suggest happened here?" Anika queried.

"I don't know."

There was a grunt and a high-pitched squeak followed by the rattle of a boxcar door opening. Hans shone his flashlight inside and muttered something under his breath. Then he called out, "This one is empty."

Anika walked over to where he stood and looked in. "Open them all. Go along the train and check each one."

She turned to Mark. "I have a feeling that we were not the first to come here."

Each car that they came to was the same. All empty. There was nothing left behind except the bones. Mark couldn't believe it. To have come this far only to be thwarted at the last hurdle. Anika flashed the light around the floor of the tunnel. The beam ran over the corpses of the long dead. Their clothes were rotted, falling away from what was left. Mark reluctantly walked over to one of them after something caught his eye. He bent down and picked it up before putting it in his pocket for later. Behind him, Anika gave a disgusted sigh and said, "Let's get out of here."

Knowing there was little chance, Mark said, "I guess you won't be needing me anymore?"

"Wrong. You come with us. Unless you want to join the bone brigade here."

Mark said, "I think I'll pass."

"Then move."

They climbed back to the top of the box car and then one by one, commenced their ascent of the vent towards daylight once more. Mark was disappointed even though he was still in his predicament. Once they were all back above ground Anika directed them to move back over the ridge. They hadn't even moved three feet before a deep voice said, "You are surrounded. Throw your weapons down."

Suddenly armed men appeared all around them. Mark looked at Anika and said, "You fucked up."

Brooke hugged him fiercely then let him go. She said, "That was a good clue you left in the castle."

"I figured that you would find it and I knew how much you hated maps being folded so I hoped it would get your attention."

"It was good thinking."

"Is Isabella alright? I hoped that she got back safely."

"She's been very worried about you," Brooke allowed. "Did you find it?"

Mark nodded. "Yes. The train is in there but there's no treasure. Someone beat us to it."

She could see the disappointment in his eyes and said, "Sorry, but, them's the breaks."

"I know that but whoever found it, killed all of those with them just as Karl Roth and Hilbert Sommer had done."

Brooke stared at him.

Mark reached into his pocket. "I got this off one of them."

He held out his hand and opened it. In his palm was an SS Death's Head skull.

"I can see your mind working, Mark," Brooke said. "What are you thinking?"

"I'm not sure. I need to think on it some more. But we have bigger problems. Actually two bigger problems. Stuber is Wolfsjunge, I'm sure that it's an assumed name passed down, and he has someone inside the Foundation."

"I know."

"Know what? Wolfsjunge or the insider?"

"That we have a mole." Brooke didn't seem impressed about either.

"Do you know who it is?"

"I have no idea," Brooke replied, shaking her head.

"What will happen to Stuber?"

"Not much, I'm afraid," Felix said as he joined them. "If his people don't turn on him then we will have nothing on him."

"So, he just gets away?" Mark said, bewildered at the prospect of the man going unpunished.

"For the time being."

"Shit."

"Forget it, Mark. He'll get what's coming to him," Brooke told him. "Right now, we have to work out where we go from here."

———

Berlin, Germany

Isabella almost crushed his ribs upon their return to Berlin. "I'm so happy to see you. Are you alright? Did they hurt you?"

"I'm fine," he told her, giving her a quick hug.

The others stood in a line, waiting their turn. Isabella stepped back, and Molly moved in to take her place, giving Mark a hug without trying to squeeze him to death. "Good to see you, old chap."

"Good to be back."

"I hear you found the train," Turow said.

Mark nodded and explained what they had discovered. "Whoever got there first, killed everyone."

Johann Schmidt said, "This is very troubling indeed. Stuber and his people are bad enough but if the treasure from the train is with another faction we've not heard about, it could mean grave danger for all of us should we continue to search for it."

"Are you saying we give up?" Brooke, incredulous, asked her employer.

"It might be the best thing we can do," Schmidt told them solemnly.

"No," Mark said. "We've come too far. I saw a list of what was on the train which had to have come from Roth. The Amber Room was on it. Which means it's still out there and we're ever so close to finding it."

Schmidt shook his head. "I'm sorry but I think it's for the best."

The whole room seemed to deflate, and a gloomy silence descended upon its occupants. Turow said, "What do you want us to work on?"

"Take a few days off. All of you and come back refreshed. I'll have something for you all to do by then."

Schmidt left them to their disappointment. "Damn it," Mark growled. "We were so close."

"It's the nature of the beast," Turow said to Mark. "I'm impressed though. You've a certain resilience about you, Mark. It'll take you a long way in this business."

Mark's head bobbed up and down as he thought about the train.

"I want you to come with me for the next couple of days," said Brooke. She noticed Isabella's expression and said, "You too, Bella, if you want."

"Where are we going?" asked Mark, his interest piqued.

"You'll see."

15

THE KELLER CONNECTION

Altes Museum, Berlin, Germany

The Altes Museum was a grand sight. The lush green lawns in front were dissected by multiple paths, some of which were centered around a fountain in the front third of the grassed area. Wide steps led up to a magnificent structure with large round pillars along its façade. Mark stood on the steps and looked up, his mouth open in awe. "I've only seen this place in pictures," he said. "It's fantastic."

"Wait until you see inside," said Brooke.

Mark glanced at Isabella. "Have you been here before?"

"So many times, I've lost count."

She looked at him briefly before grabbing his hand and began dragging him the rest of the way up the stairs. "Come on."

Inside was truly something out of this world. For Mark, anyway. He was absolutely awestruck by the sight of everything around him. At the museum's heart was a giant rotunda which stood twenty-two meters high and was capped with a cupola which had a glass skylight on top admitting natural light. The cupola itself was decorated by ornamental cassettes.

These magnificent red and gold displays showed winged spirits known as Genii, zodiac signs, plus rosettes.

Being so tall the rotunda had two floors to its structure. On the second level, set back into the wall were fourteen statues, with a further sixteen below them on the ground floor. Larger than the ones above, they sat between sturdy columns which supported the upper story. These statues were actual Roman copies of famous Greek sculptures.

During the Second World War, the museum was damaged by a bomb in 1943 and burned out in 1945. Thirteen years later the museum embarked on a restoration project, which took a further eight years.

"This is unbelievable," Mark said in a hushed voice, afraid that if he spoke too loud his voice would echo noisily.

"Isn't it though," Isabella said, her smile wide, her eyes sparkling.

"Come on," Brooke said. "Follow me. I want to show you something."

Mark and Isabella followed Brooke through the museum to a room where the walls were hung with paintings. She said to Mark, "Look around you."

"What am I looking at?"

"Just look."

Flicking his gaze over some of the paintings on the walls a picture started to develop. Portrait of Dr. Gachet by van Gogh. It was thought to have been lost forever during the war. Place de la Concorde by Edgar Degas. It too was assumed lost. Aside from the paintings, there were numerous artifacts as well. A Ming vase, handcrafted marble statues and the same in jewel-encrusted figurines.

"This is what we and other hunters across the world do," Brooke said. "Some of these things here, we found—your father found. Other artifacts were found by American hunters, some by British. Yes, things may slip through our grasp, or we may follow dead ends, but the reward is worth all of it. Do you see?"

"It's amazing."

"We'll find all there is to be found eventually, but until then, we just keep looking."

Mark looked at Brooke. "Why do you do it?"

She smiled at him. "At first it was just a job. It paid money and I didn't want to go back to the States. Then after a while, when we were finding things, I got wrapped up in the excitement and anticipation. Now, I couldn't leave even if I wanted to. It was the same with your father."

"I think I can understand it."

"You should. I can already see it in you." Brooke put her hand on his shoulder.

"But it's not just artifacts stolen in the war you look for, is it?"

"Good Lord, no," Brooke said. "Last year, Johann had us on the Yucatán Peninsula looking for ancient Mayan artifacts. That was interesting."

"I take it from the look on your face not in a good way?" Mark theorized.

"Not hardly."

"He had me in Rome looking for lost Biblical artifacts a few months back," Isabella said. "What we were looking for was found in a chamber underneath an old Roman bath house. It was just by luck we discovered them. They'd been taken from Jerusalem around the time Jesus was crucified."

"This week, stolen treasures taken by the Nazis, next week we could be in Egypt looking for the lost tomb of some pharaoh," Brooke said to him. "Everything we accomplish makes a difference."

Mark nodded. "Can we finish looking around here before we leave?"

"Go for it. I need to speak to the curator before we go anyway."

"I knew it," Mark said. "Here I was thinking you were being nice. Instead, you came here to see a guy."

Brooke's face grew dark, and she took a step forward. A broad grin split his face and he burst into laughter. "You really have to lighten up."

"I'll give you lighten up," she growled.

"Come on, Mark," Isabella said. "Let's look around."

The pair turned and walked away while behind them, Brooke watched them go, a concerned look on her face.

———

Kurt Stuber was angry. Everything he'd worked towards was starting to crumble around him. The last great thing he needed for his collection, and for the new party to come to life was the Amber Room, but it was gone. Berlin police as well as Interpol were watching him now more than ever and the people he'd hired were all behind bars.

Now he sat in the Berlin Theke, a café situated on Oranienburger Straße, waiting for his contact. While he waited, he ate Yellow Pepper Risotto and drank coffee; bitter, black, strong.

A shadow fell across the corner table, and he looked up. "You're late. Where have you been?"

"Working," Turow said. "I'm not even sure I should be meeting you out in the open like this."

"You'll do as I say," Stuber hissed.

"Not anymore. We're done. You've totally lost your mind, Stuber. First you kill the guy's father, then send men after them in Portugal, Argentina, and then kidnap him."

"He knew where the train was."

"And had you waited, I could have told you in plenty of time to get you to it before everyone else. Now, as it is, Brooke suspects—no, *knows* there is a mole in the Foundation."

"What are they doing?" Stuber asked.

"Nothing. The team is moving on to other things."

Stuber leaned forward. "What?"

"I said—"

"I know what you said. But the biggest treasure the world has ever known is still out there."

"I just follow orders," Turow said.

Stuber's hand shot across the table and locked onto Turow's arm. "Yes, my orders. You'd better get the old man to change his mind or your tenure at the Foundation will come to an abrupt end."

Turow wrenched his arm free. "How am I supposed to do that?"

"I'm sure you'll think of something."

Stuber got up from his seat, leaving whatever food was left on his plate. Looking down at his Foundation mole, he had one final thing to say. "Don't disappoint me, Turow."

———

When Turow returned to the Foundation and sought out Webster, he found him on his own at his desk. "I see you didn't take time off," Turow said.

"And do what?" the computer tech asked.

Turow shrugged. "If you feel like working then I might have something for you."

"Like what?"

"It'll be right up your alley. Something so hard that maybe you won't even be able to crack it." Turow was goading him knowing full well that Webster hated thinking of himself not up to a challenge.

"Tell me what it is."

He reached into his pocket and pulled out a list. "I have a list here of small items which would be easy to shift rather than big items."

"Are these from the train?"

"Yes."

"I thought we were letting that one go?" Webster asked.

"I hate losing."

"I'd have to go over to the dark side. It could get dangerous if I upset the wrong person."

"It's not like you haven't done it before."

"Yes, but remember, whoever took them killed all those helping. We don't even know when it was actually done. It had to be twenty or thirty years ago."

"Afraid of a little hard work?" Turow pushed a bit more.

Taking the bait, Webster said, "Hold my beer."

"You're not even old enough to drink."

"Hold my soda then."

———

Webster dropped reams of papers onto Turow's desk. "There."

Turow looked up at him open-mouthed. "What on earth?"

"They are lists of artifacts sold at underground

auctions for the past twenty years. From what I've seen, there are a couple of items on the list you gave me."

"What do you want me to do with them?" Turow asked incredulously.

"You're the document investigator; investigate."

"Damn it."

As Webster turned to walk away, he said, "Thank me later."

"Wait," Turow snapped. "What auction sites?"

"Everything you need to know is there. Good luck."

Turow began poring over the contents of the paperwork.

For the next two hours he went to work, running his finger down each page, making notes, and putting aside into various piles the ones which he thought valuable enough. Once he was through the first hundred pages he stopped and looked at what he had.

Turow had put ten aside into three piles. Of those ten, five of them stood out, sold by the same company, all dated within the past dozen years. They had been sold through an auction house in Switzerland known as Keller Antiquities. The business was owned by the Keller family; a family steeped in history and whose roots could be traced back to Poland before the war. It was a good start.

He went back to it for another two hours. It was slow torturous going and when Turow had finished, he looked at the piles again. The Keller one had grown by another five. Without doubt, that was the place to start. He dug into his pocket and took out his cell.

16

THE MOLE

Berlin, Germany

By the time the team got back to work at the Foundation a few days later, two things had happened. Stuber had a two-day head start on them, and someone had tried to murder Webster.

The young computer tech had been walking along a busy street when a car pulled up beside him, the window down, and a shooter leaned out to fire at him. As luck would have it, Webster was quick on his feet, and he dived behind a parked car just as the shooter fired.

The refuge car copped most of the punishment from the hailstorm of bullets and Webster was fortunate enough to get away without a scratch. Shaken, but unharmed.

However, Johann Schmidt was in a mood when the others arrived for their briefing.

"Would someone like to tell me why people are still trying to kill our employees?" he demanded. "Stuber is under surveillance by two agencies, so it wasn't him. Which means it was someone else. And correct me if I'm wrong, but we haven't been working on the treasure train thing for the past few days, have we?"

Silence. Mark had never seen the billionaire angry before and it wasn't pretty.

Schmidt continued. "So, tell me, what else have we been looking at that I do not know about?"

More silence.

Schmidt threw his arms in the air. "No one? People are shooting at us for no reason?"

Webster started to speak. "Sir, I—"

"I had Mister Webster looking into something which might have piqued someone's interest," Turow said.

Schmidt turned his heated gaze on him and asked stoically, "Did it not occur to you that I might need to know about it?"

"I didn't want to trouble you with it."

"What was it he was looking into?" The question came out in a hoarse, angry whisper.

"I thought of another angle for the treasure train."

If Mark thought Schmidt was angry before, he saw the man's ire grow exponentially.

But before the billionaire could explode in a volcanic rage, Turow said, "We have something. Another lead."

Schmidt swallowed to calm himself and asked, "What do you have?"

"Over the past twenty years, a Swiss auction house has been selling stolen antiquities at underground auctions throughout Europe. Webster found out about it digging around on the dark web. He probably drew some unwanted attention while he was at it."

"I still wish you'd told me about it, Greg," Schmidt said. "We were lucky we didn't lose Mister Webster. Tell me about the auction house."

"It belongs to the Keller Family—"

"Wait," Schmidt said holding up his hand to silence

Turow. "The Keller family are one of the most upstanding families in Europe."

"That's what we thought about Stuber, but we now know different," Turow pointed out. "I think that it is worth investigating. Especially now that an attempt was made on Webster's life. There must be something to it."

Schmidt turned his gaze on Brooke. "What do you think?"

"It might be dangerous. I'm willing to risk it but it'll be up to Mark."

All eyes turned to the newest member of the Foundation team. He smiled and said, "I've been shot at, kidnapped, fought off huge caimans; what else can they throw at me?"

"It'll possibly be a little more dangerous than that," Brooke said.

"How about I come too?" Turow offered.

Schmidt stared at him for a moment. He nodded. "If Brooke doesn't have any objections, then I don't see why not. Brooke?"

"I guess it'll be all right."

"Then it's settled. Greg, if you could remain behind for a moment, please."

"Yes, sir."

Once out of the meeting Mark could see the concern on Brooke's face. "What's wrong?"

"It's Turow."

"What, don't you want him to come along?"

"It's not that. He very rarely comes *along*."

"What are you thinking?" Mark asked.

"You don't want to know."

"I'm coming too, remember?"

"You know we have a mole, right?"

"Yes."

"What if it's him? What if he's the mole?" Brooke said.

"I guess it would explain why he wants to come along," Mark allowed. "But Stuber is more or less out of commission. He—"

Brooke's cell rang. "Hold that thought."

She held a finger up to silence him while she took the call. "Brooke."

Mark studied her face while she listened and spoke with whoever was on the other end. When she disconnected, she said to Mark, "I know why Turow wants to come with us."

"Are you sure?" Schmidt asked his security officer.

"Yes, sir. Interpol just reached out. He was seen with Stuber in the café."

"I don't believe it. Greg has been with me such a long time."

"You could get Webster to look into his financial accounts," Mark suggested.

The billionaire sighed. "That goes without saying. This means he's been feeding Stuber information all along."

"It looks that way, sir."

"Blast it," Schmidt growled. "This leaves us in a bit of a quandary. If I pull him off the plane to Switzerland, he'll know that something is wrong."

"Then don't," Mark said.

They both looked at him.

"Do you know what you're saying, Mister Butler?" the billionaire asked, fixing his gaze on the young man.

"Yes. If we're wrong, which is highly unlikely, you lose a good man. If it's right, then I don't think he's dangerous. He doesn't seem to be the type. If he is, I'll put a bullet in his head myself."

"No need to go that far," Schmidt said.

"You know the type, do you?" Brooke asked Mark.

"I've a fair idea after joining the Foundation. Besides, there must be a good reason."

"It's up to Brooke," Schmidt said. "She has the last say on all things to do with security."

Mark looked at her expectantly. "Well?"

"Just when I start to think you're all right, I begin to dislike you all over again."

"You like me. It's my sweet nature." Mark laughed.

"Yes, about as sweet as a lemon."

"Should I send Isabella with you instead, Brooke?" Schmidt asked drily.

"No, this one will do."

Mark raised his eyebrows as Brooke turned and started to walk out the door. *"This one* now?" he asked as he followed her out.

"That's right. I'm glad to see your ears aren't painted on."

"Unlike your tight jeans," Mark growled.

"That's it, get personal."

"You were the one who started with personal."

Their voices faded away when the office door closed, and the billionaire smiled to himself. "Never a dull moment."

Bern, Switzerland

Stuber's encrypted cell rang, and he picked it up. "What is it?"

"You need to act fast. Things are starting to fall apart."

"What do you mean?"

"Johann is sending people to Switzerland to investigate the auction house."

"Who?"

"Brooke and Butler. I managed to get on the plane so maybe I can guide their investigation somehow."

"You had better not let me down, Greg; there is a lot riding on it."

"I know, blast your eyes," Turow hissed.

"Calm yourself. I'll only put up with so much before I fix issues."

"I'm sorry."

"That's better. I am in Switzerland as we speak. Things will be taken care of."

"What about the German police? Interpol?"

"I assume they came on vacation with me."

"You're crazy."

Stuber's voice hardened. "No. Desperate. There is a difference. It tends to make people somewhat more dangerous."

On the other end Turow went silent.

"Was there anything else?" Stuber asked.

"No."

"Then don't waste my time any further."

After the call disconnected, Stuber stood on his hotel balcony and looked down at the street below, watching both vehicles and pedestrians as they passed. His eyes settled on the black Audi parked along the curb across the street. Then his eyes moved right, to a larger, dark Range Rover. His friends were still there.

He went back inside and found Meyer sitting on the large green velvet sofa. "We have a job to do tonight."

—————

The suite on the top floor of the hotel had three rooms and was lavishly decorated. Mark stood in the middle of what passed as a living room and shook his head. "I cannot believe we are staying here. In something like this."

"Just stay away from the mini-bar," Brooke warned him. "You think this room is gold-plated, just try something from there."

"That's half the fun about staying in hotels," Mark pointed out.

"Not in this one, it isn't."

They settled in and went downstairs to the restaurant for dinner, unable to get to the auction house before the following morning. Mark was further wowed by the dining room. It was large and had tall Roman pillars running up to the high ceiling which had large glass panels at its center. Marble statues were scattered around the walls as were large paintings illuminated by strategically placed picture lights.

They were shown to a table and offered a wine list. Brooke declined for them all and the waiter gave them their menus. Mark looked through his and dropped it on the table between his sparkling knife and fork. He looked puzzled but remained silent. After a while, the waiter returned to take their orders. Brooke was first and then Turow. The waiter stared at Mark who said, "Steak and fries."

"Good grief," Brooke sighed.

The waiter just stared at Mark as though he hadn't spoken at all. Mark sat there waiting for him to write the order down, but the man stared stoically at him. So, Mark added to his order. "I'd like a Coke with it as well, please."

It was a battle of wills and Mark wasn't batting an eyelid. It was the waiter who cracked first. "What would you like, sir?"

"Steak, fries, Coke."

Brooke glared at him.

"What?"

"They don't have steak and fries here."

"Is that right?" Mark asked the waiter.

"Yes, sir."

Mark nodded his understanding. "All right then. I'll have a hamburger."

"Give me strength," Brooke moaned.

"I'm just joking. I'll have the duck with plum sauce and vegetables, thank you."

"How would you like the duck cooked, sir?"

"Without its feathers preferably."

"I'll make sure the chef is notified."

"Thank you. Don't forget the Coke."

"I'll see to it, sir. Maybe one of the kitchen slaves can run down to the corner store and get it for you."

The waiter walked away, and Brooke glared at him, saying, "What was that?"

"It was a bit of harmless fun. You really should lighten up a little, Brooke."

A while later the waiter approached the table with their meals and broke up the ongoing banter. While they were eating, Turow said. "Tomorrow. I assume you have a plan, Brooke?"

"I've thought about it some, and there is an auction scheduled for tomorrow night at a place on the outskirts of Bern. Invitation only."

"Are we going?" Mark asked around a mouthful of duck.

Brooke looked at him. "Yes. I had Webster get us on the invite list. However, this will be dangerous. Make no mistake about it."

"Do we know what is on sale?" Turow asked.

"Not beforehand. It looks like they don't let anyone know until they arrive. They issue a list upon arrival."

"It should be interesting all the same," Mark said.

"We just look. Nothing stupid," Brooke warned him.

"You're the boss."

They finished their meal and went back to their suite. Later that night while Turow was asleep, Brooke found Mark out in the living room. She was dressed in a singlet top, and a pair of short pajama shorts and Mark found his gaze drawn to her tanned legs. "Can't sleep, Mark?" she asked.

"Yes. Strange bed."

"I get a bit like that. When I was deployed, I had a lot of trouble sleeping."

"Are you sure it was wise telling Turow about the auction?"

"It'll do one of two things. It'll draw him out a little more or he won't do anything with the information."

"I kind of feel sorry for him. Does he have any family?"

"I think he was married once, but not anymore. I don't know much more than that about him. I've never asked him those sorts of questions. We've always been professional."

"Do you think Stuber could be using them to get to him?" Mark asked.

"It's a possibility, I guess. It would explain why he's been feeding him information."

"I wondered how long it would take before someone figured it out," Turow said as he emerged from the shadows near his room. "What gave it away?"

Brooke and Mark turned to face him. "You were seen at a café with him by Interpol officers."

"I should have expected it, I suppose. What happens now?" he asked.

"I think you owe us an explanation," Brooke told him.

He nodded. "I heard what you said about my family.

They live in Hamburg. And, yes, Stuber knows where they are."

"Is that why?"

He nodded solemnly. "He came to me twelve months ago with what he called a proposition. It was more like an ultimatum. It really just boils down to blackmail."

"He threatened your family?"

"Yes."

"Why didn't you come to me?" Brooke asked. "Or at least go to Johann?"

"I was scared he would hurt my children."

Mark stared at him. "Did you tell them that Brooke and my father would be at Lake Toplitz?"

The pain was already evident on his face before he answered. "Yes." The word was choked off.

The anger came from within as Mark lunged towards Turow. Brooke had been expecting it and moved to intercept him.

"You got my father killed," Mark raged. "You son of a bitch. He's dead because of you."

It took all of Brooke's strength to hold Mark back. "Mark, stop it. Calm down."

"Calm down?" His eyes blazed. "He got my father killed. He got *you* shot too."

"I know, Mark, all right. I know. But we need to look at the big picture."

"What big picture would that be?"

"We can use what he knows to our advantage."

"No," Turow blurted out. "I can't help you."

"You don't have much of a choice," Brooke told him, an edge to her voice.

"They will hurt my family."

"I can have someone fetch them," Brooke offered.

"Can they keep them safe?"

"Yes."

"What do you need from me?" Turow relented, relieved that he was no longer lying to his fellow team members.

"Tell us all you know about Stuber."

———

Brooke hung up the phone and turned to Mark. "Keller Antiquities burned to the ground last night."

Mark turned his gaze on Turow. "They did this. Stuber did this."

"We don't know that for sure," he replied.

"Sure, we do."

Turow's shoulders slumped. "Yeah, I guess we do."

"What would his plan be? What does he expect to gain from it?" Brooke asked, pacing the floor, trying to put herself in Stuber's shoes.

"It would be a warning," Turow surmised.

"Warning for what?" Brooke asked.

"That they have something that he wants," offered Mark.

"Do you think he'll go after it?" Brooke asked.

"He's just proved it by burning their business down." Turow's face showed defeat.

"I guess you're right. So, what now?" Brooke shook her head, unsure of where to go next.

"I don't know." Turow hung his head.

Mark said, "Reach out to him. Find out."

Turow looked up abruptly, hesitated. "I—I can't."

"Why? Your family is safe. Brooke saw to that."

"These people are killers. They won't stop. Stuber figures he's resurrecting the Reich."

"What about the Keller family?" Mark asked.

Turow shook his head. "I don't know. As far as I know they're just dealers."

Brooke stared at him. "Call Stuber. Find out what he's up to."

Turow glanced up at her before relenting, "Alright. I'll try."

Twenty minutes later, Turow disconnected the call. He looked at Mark and Brooke who waited patiently, stoic expressions on their faces. He said, "He's going to be at the auction tonight. He wants me to keep you out of the way."

"Why is he going to be there?" Mark asked.

"The place where the auction is being held is also a warehouse where the Keller family keep a lot of their antiquities. In the office there is a cabinet. In that cabinet is a ledger—"

"Most offices have them," Brooke said impatiently.

Turow continued. "The ledger isn't like any normal ledger. It contains a list of everything that was taken from the train in the Alps."

Mark smiled. "Now we're talking."

"Is he sure?" Brooke asked, ignoring Mark's excitement.

"He sounded like he was."

"But if it isn't there, what good is the ledger?"

"The ledger also has the location."

"That's even better," Mark said. "All we have to do is get it."

"How do you propose to do that, Prometheus?"

Mark stared at her for a moment until the dime dropped. Prometheus was a Titan who supposedly stole fire from the Gods and gave it to humans. "I'm going to walk into that office and steal it before Stuber can."

Brooke closed her eyes and shook her head. "Good grief, what could possibly go wrong?"

17

THE LEDGER

Bern, Switzerland

Their invitations were checked three times before the three of them got anywhere near the door. At each verification point stood an armed guard no more than a few feet away from them.

Mark tugged at his tie, trying to loosen it to rid himself of the choking sensation he was experiencing from the pressure at his throat.

"Will you stop playing with that thing? You're only drawing attention to yourself," Brooke growled out of the corner of her mouth. She wore a long black dress which almost reached the ground, with a split up one side.

"Who ever heard of a damn warehouse holding a black-tie function?" Mark moaned. "It's a warehouse for Pete's sake."

"Shut up," Brooke hissed.

The three of them walked into the large warehouse and stopped. There were perhaps forty people inside slowly walking around, casually perusing the auction items, each of which were numbered for the convenience of matching the description on the brochure the arrivals had been supplied with. A woman approached them. She wore a red dress, and a broad diamond necklace hung about her neck. Her blonde hair was pulled back behind her ears so that the matching earrings were exposed.

She smiled showing a row of even, white teeth. Mark figured she was possibly around their age. When she spoke, her voice was soft. "Can I get you anything? A drink? Champagne?"

Mark nodded. "Yes, thank you."

"We're fine, thanks all the same," Brooke said firmly, overriding Mark's answer.

The woman gave them a warm smile. "If you do require something, just call out. I won't be far away."

The woman walked off to where an older couple stood. Watching her go, Brooke said, "That was Amy Keller."

"Who is Amy Keller?"

"She is the heiress to the Keller empire," Turow said.

"You wouldn't know they'd lost their place in the city," Mark said.

"Never fear," Turow said. "Beneath that cool exterior, is a cold and calculating businesswoman."

"Let's look around," Brooke said.

They began a slow circuit of the building, stopping to examine the items on exhibit. Each was valuable in its own right. From Egyptian relics to Greek marble carvings, to paintings which were thought stolen or lost forever. Mark said, "This is a veritable treasure trove of arts and antiquities. I don't understand how they get away with it."

"Money talks," Brooke said.

Mark seemed to accept the fact and did a sweep of the area, sighting the door with the private sign stuck to it. "Bingo."

Brooke looked to see where his gaze was directed. "Don't even think about it."

"We've got company," Turow said, his stare focused on a new arrival at the warehouse's far side entry. Brooke and Mark turned casually to look, not wanting to draw attention to themselves all staring at once. They caught on quickly when they noticed Stuber and the two people he had with him.

One of them, the man, Mark had never seen before. The woman however he knew on sight. Anika Meyer.

"Good grief, what's she doing out of jail?" he wondered out loud.

"Money talks," Brooke said again.

"We have to move quickly," Turow said. "Now that Stuber is here, he'll be wanting that ledger."

"All right, I'll—" she stopped, looking around for Mark. "Darn it, he's gone."

They both looked around to see Mark disappearing through the door marked private. Right before the rattle of automatic weapons and cries of alarm echoed throughout the warehouse.

———

Mark heard the gunfire and screams as soon as the door snicked shut behind him. Knowing that he had to work fast, he started with the large desk in front of him just as soon as he'd locked the door behind him.

He pulled open drawer after drawer in his desperate search. Each one held a myriad of paperwork, just nothing resembling what he was looking for. Mark slammed the last drawer shut in frustration and became aware of the raised voices out in the warehouse.

Mark glanced around the room and saw a filing

cabinet against the far wall. He hurried across to it and tried the top drawer. It was locked.

"Damn it," he growled. He rushed back to the desk and opened the top right drawer and started digging for a key. As luck would have it for once, he was in the right one.

The keys made a jingling sound as he held them up in front of his face. He hurried back over to the cabinet and unlocked it.

The first two drawers carried only files in manila folders. The third looked to have the same but sequestered away at the back of the drawer was a small pile of books. One just happened to be the ledger that Mark was looking for.

He opened it up and started frantically looking through. The list was enormous, the book thick. But nothing to say where the prizes were. Mark placed it on the desk and kept looking, committing to memory some of the artifacts he thought were more important than others. Not that they all weren't important. It just—he stopped.

Mark stared at the page before him, oblivious to the rattle of the doorknob as someone outside tried to get in. It was the first bang of someone trying to bust the door open which snapped him out of the trance. His eyes widened and he realized he had to do something. He tore the page free of the ledger and stuffed it down his pants. He slammed the book shut and threw it back into the filing cabinet, slamming the drawer shut just as the doorframe splintered and the door crashed back.

Mark whirled around to face the intruders. The first person through the doorway was Stuber followed by Anika Meyer.

"Well, well, well, look who we have here."

Mark's eyes darted over Stuber's shoulder as Turow

was shoved into the room by a large man carrying an automatic weapon.

Stuber continued, "It would seem that you, my friend, are here looking for the same thing we are. However, the only way that you could possibly know about it is if someone told you." He turned to look at Turow. "Isn't that right, Mister Turow?"

Turow said nothing.

"I guess others will have to pay for your indiscretion."

Turow's jaw pressed forward defiantly. "Go ahead, Stuber, you can't touch them."

"We'll see."

"He's right," Mark said. "You can't touch his family. They're under the protection of the Spezialeinsatzkommando."

This was news to Stuber, and the uncertainty flashed in his eyes for a fleeting moment. "You lie."

"Do you think he would have told us about the ledger if he thought his family were in danger?"

"Never mind," Stuber said flippantly. He signaled to his people. "Bring her in."

Anika Meyer disappeared and returned moments later with Amy Keller. She shoved the heiress into the room. Amy staggered on high heels before gathering herself and staring at Stuber defiantly. "You are scum, Stuber," she hissed.

"Come, come," he chided. "Is that any way for a lady of such high standing to speak? Oh, that's right, you and your family are just like me."

Her eyes glittered with her pent-up rage, but she remained silent.

"Now, Miss Keller, to save myself and my people a lot of unnecessary time and work, where is the ledger?"

The woman stared ahead at the opposite wall.

"No? Oh well."

Stuber took a small handgun from his pocket and nodded at Anika. Once again, she disappeared, and Mark wondered what she could be up to. A few minutes later the question was answered as she returned with a woman in her sixties wearing a black dress and diamond jewelry.

The handgun in Stuber's fist was placed against the woman's temple. "Now, shall we try again?"

Mark watched on in horror as Amy Keller set her jaw. He suddenly realized that there was no way known she was about to give Stuber the information he wanted. He saw Stuber's nod of respect and then the knuckle of the trigger finger start to tighten.

"Wait!" Mark cried out.

Surprised, Stuber turned to look at the young man. "Is there something you would like to say, Mister Butler?"

"It's in the filing cabinet."

Amy Keller hissed vehemently and Stuber knew Mark was telling the truth. The woman in the black dress stared angrily at Mark. "You young fool."

It suddenly occurred to Mark that the woman was ready to die for what the ledger held. Stuber said, "Your mother is a very brave woman."

Wow, she was about to let her mother die so the ledger wouldn't fall into Stuber's hands. Anika Meyer looked through the filing cabinet until she found the item in question. The elder Keller stared at Mark. "You have done this, and you will pay."

"It was your family who took it from the train and killed those who helped you do it. In my book, that makes you worse than Stuber. Not much but—who am I trying to kid, your family is way worse."

"And you have gotten mixed up in something you shouldn't have."

"All right," Stuber interrupted. "You two can carry on after we're gone. Greg, you'll come with us."

"What? You don't need me."

"Come now, Greg. You don't think I'm going to let you go after you betrayed me, do you?"

"But—"

Anika shoved him hard. "Move."

Mark moved but Anika was expecting it and she clubbed him with her weapon. Mark groaned and sank to the floor.

They all filed out of the room leaving Mark with the two Keller women. He looked up at them from his crouch and gave a wry smile and said, "I'd best be going too, I guess."

Amy Keller moved to block the doorway. "I don't think so. You have a lot to answer for."

Brooke appeared behind her. "Move, or you'll be made to move."

Amy turned and stared at the woman who had interrupted. "Who are you?"

"I'm his mother."

A derisive snort warned Brooke of what was about to happen, giving her the edge to be one step ahead. As Amy began moving, Brooke was already in motion. Her right hand shot forward, and she grasped Amy's arm. Mark wasn't sure what happened after that, but he was sure there was a twist and a turn in there somewhere, and before she knew what was happening, Amy Keller was flat on her back on the floor with Brooke's right high heel shoe pressing down, pinning her to the floor.

"Now," Brooke said, "what was it you were saying?"

Mark squeezed past them and looked down into the angry glare of the younger Keller. He smiled. "My ma is a real bear."

"Get going, Mark, before I leave you here."

"You won't get away with this," the older Keller growled.

"If you want us, come to the Schmidt Foundation. I'm sure Johann would be glad to see you."

They left without hinderance and once outside Brooke gave Mark a clip up the back of his head. "Ow, what was that for?"

"For going off on your own. What were you thinking?"

"What do we do about Greg?"

"You leave that to me. I gather they got the ledger?"

Mark nodded. "They did. But—"

He fished inside his pants.

Brooke pulled a face. "What are you doing?"

He took out the page he'd torn from the ledger. "I found it before they did. I don't know the location of the treasure, but I did find this."

She reached out hesitantly. "Should I sterilize it before touching? You know what, just tell me what it is."

"It's proof that the Amber Room was on the train and is with the rest of the treasure."

"All we have to do now is find it."

"Correct."

———

Berlin, Germany

"At least his family is safe," Schmidt said. "Thank goodness for small mercies."

Brooke nodded. "Felix has men taking care of them as we speak."

"Do we have any idea where they have taken him?"

She shook her head. "We're working on it."

The billionaire shifted his gaze to Mark. "What

progress are we making on the location of the missing treasure?"

"We're working on it. All we know for sure is that the room is with it."

Schmidt nodded. "Wherever it is, it would have to be big. There is a lot of treasure to be hidden."

"Could they have split it up?" Mark asked.

"It's possible but unlikely."

"What would stop the Kellers from doing something about it?" Mark asked.

"That is the million-dollar question, Mister Butler. Two parties who will do whatever it takes to keep or acquire the greatest treasure on earth."

"One actually has it."

The door burst open, and Webster filled the void. "Hang on to your hats, people. You are not going to believe this."

Schmidt's face showed annoyance at the interruption. However, he let it go, saying, "Believe what, Mister Webster?"

"The Kellers have no idea where the treasure actually is."

"What?" Mark gasped. "How can that be?"

"Yes, Mister Webster, how can that be?"

"You'll have to bear with me because this gets a little complicated and long-winded but it's all worth it."

"Well then, how about we gather the team, and you can tell us all together."

————

"Old man Keller—"

"Who is 'Old Man Keller', Mister Webster?" Schmidt asked. "Names and facts, please Mister Webster. Names and facts."

"Elmar Keller," Webster replied grudgingly. "Wehrmacht Colonel Elmar Keller."

"Thank you, Mister Webster, continue."

Webster ran his gaze over the rest of those gathered in the conference room. "Elmar Keller worked in Hermann the German's office in—"

"Mister Webster—"

"Hermann Göring."

"Thank you."

"He worked in Hermann Göring's office towards the end of the war. He was a decorated soldier who served on the Eastern Front before being transferred to Western Europe after the allies invaded. However, he was wounded in France and sent back to Germany to recuperate. It was there he was singled out to work for Hermann the—Hermann Göring. This would have brought him into direct contact with Karl Wolff and presumably the hordes of treasure and all the hiding places where the stuff was all stashed. Including the train."

"How do you know all this?" Mark asked.

"It wasn't easy."

"Continue, Mister Webster."

"So, eventually as the war was in its final phases, Göring started to hide everything that he could, assuming that once the war was over, he could come back to it. Unknown to him, he was bound to stretch rope. However, we know he took cyanide before that happened."

"Was Keller in league with Wolff?" Brooke asked.

"Not as far as I can tell," Webster replied. "But he was still in the position to pick up stray bits of intel and put it all together. When the train left, he'd gathered enough to know where they were taking it. He just waited to see what was going to happen and when Wolff died, he decided to act. Not straight away of course because different Monuments Men groups were still searching for all kinds of missing treasures. But eventually he did, and we all know how that ended for the ones who helped him. He also made the secret ledger which was passed on to his family."

"But what about the location?" Isabella asked.

"That's just it. The location was put in code into the ledger and the only one who knew the key was the old man."

"He never told anyone?" Molly asked.

"No. I'm sure he meant to, but he died suddenly before he could."

"So, the ledger is useless," Mark observed.

"Without the key, yes."

"Was there anything on the reverse side of that page I pulled out of the ledger which has made it onto the black market?" Mark asked.

Molly said, "I searched every database I could think of and came up with nothing so, as far as I could tell, what was on that train is still all together wherever it was hidden."

"So, what have the Kellers been selling all these years?" Mark asked.

"Bits and pieces that have been found over time and not declared."

"It must have annoyed them no end knowing they were sitting on a fortune and had no way of finding it," Brooke said.

"This is your mission, Jim, should you choose to accept it," Mark said.

Everyone looked at him questioningly. He waited for someone to say something. When no one spoke he said, "Come on, people, Mission Impossible. Surely you all know it."

Everyone looked at Schmidt.

"You're kidding," Mark muttered.

"So, how do we find it?" the billionaire asked his charges.

"It would have to be somewhere large to store it," Isabella said. "The drier the better."

"Remember all those years ago when the Yanks found that store at the end of the war in the Altaussee salt mine?" Molly said. "They were sorting it out for years."

"Something like that would be dry enough," Krause said. "You'd need something big like that for what was on the train."

Schmidt thought for a moment. "Molly, find what you can about Elmar Keller's youth. Where he was born, brought up, things like that. Work with Mister Webster on it."

"Yes, sir."

"Werner, I want you to find out who he served with during the war, where his regiment or whatever it was, was stationed. Maybe something will intersect with it."

"I'll see to it."

"Brooke, reach out to the German police and Interpol and see what has become of Greg. Get an update for me."

"Yes, sir."

"What about me?" asked Mark.

"You saw the ledger, yes?" Schmidt asked.

"I did. Well, some of it, anyway."

"Work with Isabella. Get down whatever you can remember."

"Yes, sir. I'll try."

"You've got until this time tomorrow to come up with results. Let's find something."

18

THE AUSTRIA CONNECTION

Stuttgart, Germany

Stuber was far from happy. His people had been looking over the ledger and so far, had come up with nothing. He glared at Anika. "What are they doing? Are they stupid? Do I need to get someone else to look at it?"

"There is nothing in the ledger to say where the treasure is hidden," she explained. "If there was, they would have found it by now."

"So, it is useless? We went to all that trouble for a useless book?"

"It would appear so. However, there was something they observed."

"What?"

"There appears to be a page missing."

Stuber sighed. It was the sound made by someone frustrated about being surrounded by fools who could do nothing right. "There was a page missing. Of course, there was a page missing! I bet you any amount of money that *schwein* took it before he told us where the blasted thing was." He chuckled. "That was how he knew where it was. Good grief he played us for fools. I'm starting to wish that I had disposed of him when I had the chance. There is every chance that Schmidt and his band of merry men already know where it is."

"I don't think so, sir."

Stuber got out of his seat and paced the great hall where he'd been enjoying his midday meal. When they had left Bern, he and his people headed for Stuttgart where he had a large estate outside of the city. It was here that he hoped to reorganize and make plans for the retrieval of the treasure. The billionaire looked at Anika. "Something isn't right."

"Why?"

"You had a team watching the Kellers to inform us if they made a move to get the treasure before us, didn't you?"

"Yes."

"Have they moved at all?"

"No."

"Now do you see what I mean?" Stuber asked.

"They haven't moved because they don't know where the treasure is either," Anika said. "They never did."

"Exactly. What makes it more puzzling is why that kid would tear out a page from the ledger."

Anika thought for a moment. "I think I know what was on that page."

"Please, enlighten me." The sarcasm was thick.

"The Amber Room."

––––––––

Berlin, Germany

"Tell me what you have for me," Schmidt said to his people as they all gathered around the table.

"Keller was raised in Austria," Krause said so everyone could hear. "Right up until he moved with his family to Berlin at the height of Hitler's power."

"Where in Austria?" asked Schmidt.

"Hallstatt," Krause answered his boss.

"Bingo," Molly said. "He served in the area with a German Mountain Division early in the war before they were transferred east to the Russian Front."

"You think salt mines?" Schmidt mused.

"There are a few," Krause added with a nod.

"Then this would be a good place to start," Schmidt observed.

"Without doubt a good place indeed," Krause concurred.

"What else do we know?" Schmidt asked, wanting input from anyone in the room who had something to say.

"Interpol arrested the Keller family last evening," Brooke said. "Most of the ones involved with their black-market activities anyway."

"That's something. Take them off the board and all we have to worry about is Stuber and his newly rebuilt army," Mark said. "Do we know how Anika Meyer got out?"

Schmidt shook his head. "No but you can assume that it came from somewhere in the government."

"He's that well connected, huh," Mark opined.

"I'm afraid so. But since there is an increased threat to our safety, I have hired some extra security to help out." Schmidt stood and looked towards the end of the hall.

As if on cue, the door to the hall opened and in walked Felix flanked by two other men from the Spezialeinsatzkommando. The big man looked at Mark and winked. "Brooke tells me you need a strong hand to keep you in line."

Mark looked at the big man and smiled.

"You all know Felix, I gather?" Schmidt said.

Everyone nodded so Schmidt continued, "He and his men will be extra security. Brooke will still be in charge. All of us are going to Austria this afternoon. Get everything you need packed and be ready to fly by four. Understood? We're not coming back until we find that treasure."

Everyone started to rise when Schmidt pulled Brooke to one side. "Has there been any news about Greg?"

"Nothing, sir. We don't even know if he's still alive."

"Thank you. Keep checking."

Stuttgart, Germany

"I have news," Anika said to her boss while he sat on the sunlounge by the sparkling clear pool.

"It had better be good, Anika, because I'm about all out of patience," Stuber growled in a low voice.

"Johann Schmidt has put every one of that team of his onto the foundation plane and shipped them off to Austria."

He raised his eyebrows. "Really? Where?"

"Salzburg."

"There could only be one reason why he would shift everyone to Salzburg. He knows where the treasure is."

"It's quite possible."

"Get everyone together. We've got a plane to catch."

"What about Turow?" Anika asked.

"Bring him with us."

Austria

The hotel was a wonderful piece of architecture. From marble pillars to the matching marble floors. The ceiling of the foyer had gold gilding around a large, central, hand-painted mural. The team was split up into their own separate rooms for the duration of their stay.

The following morning, Mark, Brooke, and Felix were headed into the mountains to the lakeside town of Hallstatt. There they would search for anything, any clue that might lead them to the prize that they sought. The others would remain behind in Salzburg where they could use every scrap of technology at their disposal to help in any way they could.

The morning after their arrival, Mark, along with Brooke and Felix, drove to Hallstatt to commence their mission. First though they checked into a hotel/chalet style hotel where they would base themselves. They had just finished unpacking when Brooke's cell rang.

"Hello."

"Brooke," Molly Roberts said on the other end in Salzburg. "I've got someone for you to meet. He's an old salt miner and he knows all the mines like the back of his hand."

"Send me his details, Molly, and we'll check in with him. There's still enough daylight left."

A few minutes later, the cell pinged, and Brooke checked out the information on the screen. Locking her room, she walked the short distance down the hallway to the next door along. She knocked and Mark came to the door with a towel wrapped around himself and no shirt. He appeared to be about to get in the shower. "Get your kit on, it's time to go. We've got a lead."

He nodded. "Be right with you."

Next, she roused Felix and told him what they were

doing. The big commando went back into his room and emerged with a backpack. Not long after that, Mark joined them in the corridor.

They took the elevator down to the lobby and outside to the lot where they got into a Mercedes SUV and drove away. Within a few heartbeats, a dark colored Audi pulled onto the street and began tailing them.

———

"Someone is following us," Felix said as he looked in the rearview mirror. "They're driving a dark Audi."

Brooke dropped the sun visor, using the mirror sequestered there, moving it so she could see out the back window. "I've got it."

Mark risked a glance over his shoulder and saw a white SAAB behind them but no dark colored Audi. "Are you sure it's back there?"

"It's there," said Felix. "What do you want to do, Brooke? The place we want isn't far away."

"Keep going past it. Take them out of town and see if we can lose them."

"All right, you're the boss."

The accelerator went down, and the SUV shot forward. Felix came to a T-intersection and jammed on the brakes. The Mercedes decelerated rapidly, and the big commando swung on the wheel. He turned right, cutting off a car coming down the street in the opposite direction, narrowly missing it.

Mark braced himself in the back while holding his breath as the Audi went past. He looked out the window and saw the female driver, eyes wide with shock. Felix gave the vehicle more gas and Mark felt the rear end kick out a little.

He looked back over his shoulder at the intersection

and saw the Audi appear, taking the turn sideways. It was falling behind as the SUV gathered speed. "He's still back there," Mark said.

Felix just grunted as he came to another sharp turn. Dropping the Mercedes down a gear, he swung violently on the wheel. Mark felt as though his body would slide across the rear seat, but the restraining belt held him firmly in place.

Suddenly the SUV felt like it was beginning to climb. Mark looked out the front window and saw that the road had narrowed and was rising. They came to the first tight corner, and he realized that they were definitely going up.

Mark looked out the back window once again and saw that the Audi had closed the gap between them significantly. He saw the driver and the passenger. The latter leaned out the window and aimed a handgun in the vehicle's general direction. Then the Audi disappeared as Felix put the Mercedes into another tight corner. Mark called out, "The passenger has a gun."

"Keep your head down then," Brooke said.

Mark took out his Glock 19 and chambered a round.

Felix gave the Mercedes more gas out of the corner and the vehicle shot forward. Behind them the Audi turned into the bend and like the SUV, accelerated out of it. The man appeared once more at the passenger window with his weapon. This time he fired. A loud clang in the rear of the SUV rattled the interior as the first round struck home. It was quickly followed by a second and third round.

"This worm is annoying me," Felix growled as he threw the Mercedes into another turn.

Mark rolled down his window.

"What are you doing?" Brooke snapped at him.

"Shooting back," he replied. "I'm with Felix, these guys are annoying."

Outside the SUV, on the left, the road ended, and the shoulder dropped away sharply down an embankment that ran that way for a good two-hundred feet. The drop disappeared momentarily as the Mercedes drove through a cut then out the other side.

Mark unclipped the seatbelt and leaned out the window and fired three shots. All flew wide and the shooter in the Audi fired back. Bullets hit the rear of the SUV and Mark muttered something incoherent under his breath.

Felix took another sharp turn and the pursuing vehicle disappeared again before reappearing as they came out the other side of the corner. Mark fired another handful of shots, seeing a couple strike home.

The driver swerved back in behind the SUV, so Mark didn't have a clear field of fire.

Flying up behind the SUV, the Audi rammed into the back of it. The Mercedes shuddered but remained on the road. Mark heard Brooke growl something to Felix and the big commando did something unexpected. He stomped on the brakes.

The speeding Audi was forced to take evasive action and it swung around them. But Felix was watching and as they started to pass, he trod on the gas and swerved to the right.

The front fender where it wrapped around the corner of the quarter panel hit the Audi in the rear quarter panel and kicked the back of the speeding vehicle out. The driver lost control and before he knew it the Audi had gone over the edge of the embankment and become a ton of runaway freight train as it plowed down the slope.

Felix stopped the SUV and backed up. They climbed out and walked to the edge of the slope and stared down.

The passage of the vehicle was marked by plowed ground which scarred the gradient, leaving deep brown furrows in its wake.

At the end of the path was the Audi, battered, bent, and upside down. Mark saw some movement from the wreck and the two occupants staggered from it, obviously feeling effects not only of the impact with the Mercedes, but of the violent descent and inversion.

Felix reached into his pocket for his cell. While he talked, Mark saw the two people stagger away from the wreck and go further down the slope as they tried to put distance between themselves and the vehicle before trouble showed up. Felix disconnected and said, "The police will be here soon."

Brooke said, "Let's go then."

"We should stay here," the big commando pointed out.

"We've got a meeting to get to."

"You go," said Felix. "I'll get someone to drop me off when I'm done here."

Brooke shrugged. "Suit yourself. I'll let Johann know what happened."

Mark and Brooke climbed into the slightly damaged SUV and carefully made their way back down the mountain.

———

Rene Ebner lived in a small house with two bedrooms. He was a bent-over man in his seventies with silver hair and a lined, leathery face which looked to be tough, comparable to what he came across as being. He invited them in and offered coffee which they both declined. Then he asked in his gruff way, "What do you want?"

It was nothing personal and Brooke knew it. She said, "We think you might be able to help us with something."

"What?"

"Have you ever heard of the Keller family. Elmar Keller in particular?"

The old man's eyes narrowed. "I have heard of him."

"What can you tell us about him?"

"In the early days he was involved in salt mining," Rene explained. "He had three mines in the mountains. That was before he started dealing in stolen antiquities."

"How do you know they were stolen?" Mark asked, interested to find out how much the old man knew about the treasure.

"When artifacts and paintings that were stolen by the Germans keep turning up at his auction houses, then you know he's up to no good."

"How did he get away with it?" Mark asked.

"Money. He paid off whoever it took."

"Do you know where he kept it all?"

Rene shrugged. "No idea."

"Have you ever heard any whispers about a Nazi gold train?"

His shoulders rose and fell again. "Sure, who hasn't?"

"It was found."

"Really?"

"Yes, but it was empty. Someone got to it before we did."

"And you think Keller was that person?" Rene asked.

Brooke said, "We're sure of it."

"Well, there you go." The old man rubbed his head.

"He killed those who helped him. The authorities are trying to identify remains that were found."

The old man looked thoughtful. "Do you know when this happened?"

"It's hard to tell. A while back. We won't know exactly until tests are completed."

Rene nodded. He rose unsteadily from his chair and shuffled out of the room. Mark and Brooke looked at each other, confused. When he returned, there was something in his hand. It was a newspaper clipping. "Here, have a look at this. It may be nothing. Or it may be something."

Mark moved closer to Brooke. The clipping was from a local newspaper dated in the seventies. The headline talked about a tragic collapse in a salt mine where everyone below ground, apart from a couple of men, were killed. Mark looked up at Rene. "Was this one of Keller's mines?"

"It was. My brother was killed in that collapse. The only ones to escape were Keller, his foreman, and another worker whose name I forget. Anyway, it doesn't matter, they're all dead. The foreman died two months after the collapse and the worker a month later. Car accident."

Mark looked at Brooke. "Are you thinking what I am?"

"It's a good way to cover up a mass murder," she allowed. She looked at Rene. "Did they ever retrieve the bodies for their families to bury?"

He shook his head. "No. They're still in there."

Mark said, "I bet there are no bodies at all, and it is all a fake."

"Are you saying that there was no cave-in?" the old man asked.

"Yes. Has anyone ever been up there?"

"No. Once the disaster happened it was sealed off by Keller. They put a plaque up and nobody ever went back."

"What about his family?" asked Brooke.

"Not even them."

"There was no investigation?"

"Only done by Keller."

"Can you show us on a map how to get there?" Mark asked Rene.

"You want to go there?" The old man seemed surprised.

"Yes, sir. And I'll tell you right now, your brother is not buried in that mine."

19

THE MINE

Welle eins, Austria

"Do you think we should have waited for Felix?" Mark asked Brooke.

"He could still be some time, what with waiting for the authorities and who knows what they will want him to do," she replied. "Besides, we're only going for a look. Nothing more. Once we've seen it, we report back, and Johann can decide what he wants to do next."

The SUV took another sharp corner before commencing another climb. The road was in a state of disrepair from years of neglect. The single lane thoroughfare had serviced the mine site, but with the mine being defunct, the access road had not been maintained for many years.

The Mercedes lurched as its front left wheel dropped into what felt like an asteroid crater. Mark's shoulder hit the door pillar and he winced. "You want me to drive?"

Brooke glanced at him in disbelief. "No."

"Then, would you?"

"Like you could do better. Have you seen the state of this road?"

"I'm just saying." Mark wrapped his hand tighter around the panic handle above him.

"Well don't," Brooke growled.

Suddenly the road stopped, blocked by a large fence with two signs on it. Both were warning trespassers to keep out. Brooke and Mark climbed from the Mercedes and walked forward. Mark said, "I guess we go the rest of the way on foot."

"I guess so," Brooke agreed. "Wait here."

She walked back to the Mercedes and returned with her backpack.

"Let's find us a way in," Brooke said.

"Yes, boss."

Mark made his way along the fence until he found a hole. He looked back at Brooke and motioned her with his hand, saying, "Over here."

She joined him and he pointed at the hole in the chain-link fence. "After you."

"Are you being a gentleman all of a sudden?" Brooke asked disbelievingly.

"No. But if there is a big dog on the other side then he's going to need something to chew on."

She chuckled and shook her head. "Where is that bravado of yours?"

"When it comes to man-eating guard dogs, I don't have any."

She leaned down and started through the hole. "Come on then."

They walked up the road which was lined by tall pines. The air was filled with the sweet aroma of pine sap. The mountain breeze held a unique coolness, yet it wasn't cold. They continued climbing the low rise until it flattened out, a plateau spreading out before them, surrounded on two sides by steep cliffs. In front of them stood an old walled-up opening, bordered by an arch that resembled an old railway tunnel. This was the original entrance to the mine. They walked up to it and stood staring at the obstruction. "How are we going to get around this?" Mark asked.

"There has to be another way in," Brooke said. "Or…"

She walked closer to the wall and studied it. From where he stood it appeared to be solid concrete. Brooke rapped on it with her knuckles before shaking her hand. "It's definitely solid."

She ran her hand along the wall stopping to examine some of the pitting which had occurred over many years of sun, rain, and snow. She reached the left side of the arch and stopped. She shook her head and repeated her movements until reaching the right side. Mark said, "Anybody would think we're in a stupid Indiana Jones movie."

"Are you saying those movies were stupid?" Brooke asked without turning around.

"No, but what you're doing—" He stopped as she walked three feet beyond the outline of the arch and pulled away some of the undergrowth that had grown up. She fiddled around with something and without warning the concrete wall began to slide back. She turned and smiled at Mark. "Indiana Jones taught me a lot."

He shook his head. "I—I have nothing to say."

Brooke dug into her backpack and took out a couple of small flashlights. She tossed one to Mark. "Let's go find out what's in here."

————

The inside of the mine was filled with old, musty air that had been trapped inside for the forty plus years it had been sealed. Mark wrinkled his nose at the offensive smell. "This is crazy."

"Why? I thought you wanted to find this treasure."

"I do, but there's something telling me this is a bad idea."

"We can always go back," Brooke said giving him the option.

"Are you kidding? And miss the find of the century? Let's keep going."

The tunnel seemed to grow narrower as they moved along it. It was, however, an optical illusion, just a trick of the light on the scarified walls. They went deeper until the tunnel stopped. Before them was a large elevator made of steel. Brooke tried the gates and they screeched back on dry rollers. The high-pitched shriek seemed to fill the void they were in, and Mark winced. Beyond the gates was an elevator cage large enough to fit a small car.

They shone their flashlights around it, inspecting the interior. Mark's light stopped on a panel and box on the far wall. "I wonder if it still works?"

"I doubt it," Brooke replied.

Before taking the first step into the elevator, one thing went through his mind. *I hope this thing is safe.*

Then he stepped forward.

He felt it move under his weight and held his breath. For a moment he imagined it would plummet from beneath him, taking him screaming hundreds of feet to his death. Mark let out a slow breath of relief. He took another step forward and brought his feet together.

"What are you doing?" Brooke hissed.

"Going to check the electrical box."

"You fool. Do you actually think it will still work after all these years?"

"Only one way to find out," Mark replied nervously licking his lips.

He took another couple of steps, the elevator shifting with his movements. Brooke said, "Even if by some miracle it does work, what do you propose to do?"

Mark chuckled nervously. "I haven't thought that far ahead."

A couple more steps and he'd reached it.

Mark unlatched the cover and swung it wide. Inside were three buttons. UP, DOWN, and STOP. He reached out; his index finger extended.

"Wait!" Brooke exclaimed.

He looked back at her. "What?"

"What if it works?"

"Do you really think it'll work after all this time?"

"What if it does?"

"Then I guess I'll go down," he said with an uncertain grin.

"You're a fool," Brooke said and stepped cautiously into the elevator. "Press it."

The straightened finger pressed the button. The gates closed and the elevator began to move.

———

"This is exciting," Mark said, giving Brooke the stupid grin once more. He flicked his flashlight around the elevator. "I hope we don't run out of battery."

"It's a bit late to worry about that now, don't you think, genius?"

"I was just saying."

The elevator slowed and stopped with a spongy bounce. "I just thought of something else," Mark said.

"What?"

"I hope it goes back up."

"You're just full of happy thoughts, aren't you?" Brooke said drily.

She slid the gates back and they stepped out onto solid ground. Stretched out before them was a tunnel. Wide but only around twelve or thirteen feet high. "Did you ever see that movie where those cavers got trapped in a cave—*Descent* I think it was called?"

Brooke had and it had scared the living daylights out of her. "You do know you're never going to see daylight again, right?" she growled at Mark.

"What did I do?"

"Just keep walking."

They continued along the tunnel until it stopped and turned to the right. They followed it for another twenty or thirty feet before it turned back to the left. As they rounded the corner they stopped. Their eyes grew wide, and their jaws dropped before eventually turning into broad smiles. "Holy shit," Mark gasped.

There before them was a great man-made cavern, the roof held up by large pillars like those seen in ancient Rome. And there, piled high throughout was crate after crate after crate of what one could only assume were artifacts from the treasure train.

Mark said. "We found it. We actually found it."

"And I must thank you for doing so."

Mark and Brooke turned to see an old friend standing behind them. Kurt Stuber.

20

THE EGGS

"How long will it take you to get it all out of here?" Stuber asked.

Anika shrugged. "Ten, twelve hours."

"That's far too long. They will be missed before then and people will start looking."

"You forget the only one who knew where they were going has been taken care of," Anika reminded him.

"Fine. Have the charges put in place while you are at it."

"It will be done."

Mark looked worried. "What charges?"

"The ones to collapse the mine, of course," Stuber said with an evil smirk.

"Oh."

"I'm sorry I won't be here with you, but I have a prior engagement."

"You're scum, Stuber," Brooke hissed at him.

A man hurried towards them, an excited expression on his face. "It's here. We found it."

"Found what?" Mark asked, his curiosity piqued.

Stuber smiled. "Come with us and you will see."

The man led them back into the large cavern to a huge stack of crates. He said, "It had been broken down, but it's here."

One of the crates was open. Stuber looked inside. He smiled. A grin almost as wide as the cavern itself. He beckoned to Mark and Brooke with a wave of his hand. "Come."

They stepped forward and looked inside. Mark's eyes widened in awe and wonder as he took in the panel that was illuminated by the false light. "It's...amazing."

"Isn't it?"

Mark reached out to touch it but a stern growl from Stuber halted his hand. "I don't think so."

Mark looked at Brooke. "If he's going to kill us, you'd think he'd let me at least touch it. Grant me a dying wish?"

Brooke shrugged. "He might think you'll break it."

"The Germans totally dismantle it, and he thinks I'll break it. What a dick."

"Enough!" Stuber snarled. "Take them away and keep an eye on them."

Mark and Brooke were led away to a darkened corner of the cavern where they were kept under observation by one of Stuber's men. They watched on as the treasure thieves slowly emptied out the room.

As the time slipped by, the guard assigned to keep an eye on them grew disinterested and eventually moved away from where he was supposed to be situated. Mark turned to Brooke when he was out of earshot. "What are we going to do?"

"I don't know."

"I thought you always had a plan?"

"I do," she replied. "Stay alive."

"If they blow this place up with us still down here, I think that might be a little hard."

"I'm working on it."

Mark sighed and then focused his gaze on a small crate atop a couple of others. He shrugged. "What the heck."

He made his way cautiously towards it. Behind him, Brooke whispered, "What are you doing?"

"Looking."

"Get back here."

Mark ignored her and looked the small wood crate over. He tried to get his fingers under the lip of the top and pry it upwards. However, it wasn't moving. He looked around and saw nothing thin enough to use.

Then he spotted a rock. With a shrug of his shoulders, he muttered. "Might do."

Mark bent down and picked it up. Then looked at the crate once more before using the rock, thrusting up to try and knock the lid free. The trick was not to make too much noise.

He hit it once, the sound seemed deafening when in fact it wasn't much more than a dull thud. He glanced at Brooke again. She glared at him and mouthed words which he didn't want to think about.

Mark went back to the task at hand and tried again. Using more force this time, the blow was much louder, and he glanced to see if it had alerted their guard. He was gone. Relief flooded through him, and he gave the lid another whack, this time somewhat harder than the last.

The lid lifted a touch and Mark suddenly felt encouraged by the sight. He hit it again and it lifted some more. Dropping the rock, he went to work with his hands once again. This time the lid started to come away. With gritted teeth, Mark put all his strength into it and the top of the crate came free.

From the light of the lamps spread throughout the cavern he could see that the crate was filled with straw.

Mark reached down into it and felt something under his fingers. Nothing big but smaller, delicate. He wrapped his fingers around it and lifted the object free.

Mark's eyes widened. In his hand he held a small Faberge Egg. It was white and gold and a color that Mark guessed was platinum. Small clusters of diamonds caught the light. "Holy cow," Mark breathed. He was holding Alexander III Commemorative Faberge Egg, listed as missing since before the Russian Revolution.

Mark hurried over to where Brooke sat. "Look!" he exclaimed. "Look what I found."

Brooke's eyes darted around the cavern. "Shh! Do you want everyone to hear?"

"Do you know what this is?" he asked.

"I know what it is," she whispered back in a harsh tone. "What are you going to do with it?"

Mark picked up the small pack he'd brought with him and put the egg inside. He then hurried back to the crate and put straw in on top of it. Brooke joined him and she delved her hands beneath the top layer until she found something else.

Bringing her hand clear she held the object up so they could both see it. Another egg. This one was prettier than the one Mark had found, and she knew it by sight from pictures she'd seen of it. Enamel and gold surface, small stones, small heraldic lions and a royal arms symbol. It was the Royal Danish Faberge Egg.

"Good Lord," Brooke gasped.

The egg followed the other one into Mark's pack before they both were sifting through the straw in the crate looking for more.

What they came up with was the egg from Cherub with Chariot, Hen with Sapphire Pendant, and the Faberge Egg called Mauve. All went into the bag and were covered with straw to keep them safe. Then Mark put the lid back on.

"Now you've got them, smarty pants," Brooke said. "How do you propose to get them out?"

"I don't know. Any ideas?"

"Not a one."

Salzburg, Austria

"They've been missing for seven hours," Johann Schmidt said worriedly. "I don't like it."

"I tried to meet the contact, but he's disappeared. So, whatever he told them is an unknown quantity," Felix supplied.

"Damn it."

"I'm not sure what else to do."

Molly appeared. "I think I might have found something."

"What is it?"

"I have a list of the mines owned by the Kellers." She passed it to Felix.

He said, "I have a contact who may be able to narrow the search."

Schmidt nodded. "Do it."

Felix left the billionaire and his young charge in the room together. Molly looked at her boss and asked, "Do you think they'll be alright?"

"I hope so, Molly, I certainly hope so."

"Hope what?"

They turned to see Isabella standing in the doorway. Schmidt said, "We were just talking about finding the treasure."

"No, you weren't. You were talking about Mark and Brooke. Has there been some news?"

"We've heard nothing yet."

"Would you tell me if you did?" she demanded.

Molly could see the girl's façade starting to crumble and she moved to put her arm around Isabella's shoulders. "Take it easy, Bella. I'm sure they'll be fine. Felix is doing everything he can to find them. I'll bet by this time tomorrow, they'll be right here with us."

"I wish I could believe you, Molly. But I have a bad feeling about this."

———

Welle eins, Austria

The last of the treasure was loaded onto the trucks at the top of the mine. Meanwhile down below, Stuber waited for his right-hand woman to join him and his prisoners. When she did, Mark and Brooke were surprised to see Turow with her.

"Are you alright, Greg?" Brooke asked.

"Yes, my family?"

"They're safe."

"What happens now?" Mark asked.

Stuber gave him a cold smile. "This is where we part ways. The charges have been placed in such a way that when they go off, the mine will fill with water from an underground spring."

"Great," said Mark forcing a smile. "We get to drown. I always wondered what that was like. Maybe you could hang around and we could find out together. Or you, Anika? I'd like to hold your hand as we die together."

"As sweet as it sounds, I will have to pass," Anika replied.

"Pity. I'll miss not seeing you take your last breath."

"Enough. It is time we were leaving, Anika." Stuber looked at his watch. "You may have ten minutes left before—" he held his hands in fists and then opened them to simulate an explosion. "Boom."

"I'll make the most of the time I have left," Mark said, his voice dripping with sarcasm.

"Goodbye."

They retreated towards the elevator, climbed aboard, closed the gate, and went up into the darkness.

"Oh well," Mark said, "at least they left the lights for us. And they never took the eggs."

"Eggs? What eggs?" Turow asked.

"The lost Faberge eggs."

"You have them?" he asked, his eyes going wide.

"Shame they'll be lost with us then."

"Not if I can help it," Brooke said and started towards where the first lot of explosives was situated. She looked at it sadly and shook her head.

"Can you do anything with them?" Mark asked.

She shook her head again. "I'd have to disable the timer. But doing that would set off the failsafe which can sense it and the bomb will explode. If I try to disable that then there is a mercury trigger which if moved only slightly will make the bomb explode. And if I try—"

"All right, I get it. We're screwed."

"Not yet," Brooke snapped. "While we breathe there is a chance. Come with me."

They hurried over to the elevator shaft and Brooke opened the metal gates. She stood inside and looked up the pitch-black shaft. "You have to climb up there, Mark."

"Me? What about you?"

"There is not time for all of us to go. You can climb up there and lower the elevator to get us."

"It must be over five-hundred feet," Mark pointed

out. "I'll not be able to see a thing. Even if I could, I'd never make it before the bomb exploded."

Brooke's shoulders slumped. "That's great."

"What is?"

"I got your dad killed and now you."

Mark chuckled nervously. "If it makes you feel any better, I don't blame you."

"I'm going to miss my family," Turow said.

"Your wife hates you," Brooke said.

Turow burst out laughing. "You're right. She does. But my children—"

A dark silence descended upon them as they started to accept that their lives were suddenly about to be cut short.

"No," said Mark. "No, no, no. This isn't how it ends."

"What are you on about?" Brooke asked.

"These mines, I read somewhere that some of them had another way out."

"I don't know where you read that," Brooke said. "But it sounds like a dream to me."

"Dreams are about all we have at the moment."

"We're five-hundred feet down, Mark," Brooke reminded him.

"Yes, but we're on a mountain."

"Uh, huh."

"I tell you what. If I find a way out, you cook me dinner for a week."

"If you find a way out, I'll cook your dinner for a year."

Mark reached into his pocket and took out a book of matches. He broke one off and lit it. Brooke sighed, "Great, we're about to die and you're playing with matches."

For a moment nothing happened. Then there was a faint flicker of movement in the flame as it leaned to the right. Mark looked left. "That way. Do you still have your flashlight?"

"I do."

"Then let's go."

"Mark—"

"We've got nothing to lose, Brooke," Turow pointed out. "We stay here the blast will more than likely kill us. We follow whatever it is and don't make it, then we drown."

"All right, let's go," she sighed. "Just so you know, I hate water."

"That's all right," Mark told her. "I hate the dark."

21

THE LONG WAY DOWN

Welle eins, Austria

They found a narrow tunnel at the rear of the cavern. It was around ten feet wide and approximately the same high. They hurried as best they could but after a few hundred feet they suddenly realized that the tunnel was taking them further down.

"This is working well," Brooke noted.

Mark stopped and lit another match. "The breeze is still there."

Brooke looked at her watch. "So is that bomb and it's due to go off in a couple of minu—"

BOOM!

The explosion was almost deafening in the enclosed area under the mountain. Brooke looked back over her shoulder and saw the rolling wave of orange flames roaring along the passage. "Run!" she cried out.

Mark and Turow did as ordered but they hadn't gone far before Brooke cried out once more. "Take a deep breath and get down."

No sooner had they dived to the hard passage floor

when the orange wave washed over them, the heat intense. Mark kept holding his breath while around them the flames ate all the oxygen the passage held.

Then came the rumbling like an earthquake or a truck coming towards them. Mark looked back and saw in the dim torch light the wall of water coming towards them.

It hit them like a freight train. Mark felt himself tumble over and over in the darkness of the tumult. He hit something and felt a rib give under the impact. He cried out, and foul-tasting water flooded into his mouth. He coughed and jerked as he tried to bring air into his lungs, but it was an impossible task. Suddenly Mark realized that he was dying and there was nothing he could do about it. Then he closed his eyes and the darkness engulfed him.

———

"Mark, wake up!"

The darkness started to fade to grey light. His chest heaved and air rushed into his lungs.

"Come on Mark, darn it," Brooke growled. "Wake up or you'll kill us both."

His eyes flew open, his legs flailing in mid-air. Mark looked down and saw the sheer vertical drop of the cliff face stretched out a thousand feet below. To his right, water fell in sheets towards the jagged rocks at the bottom.

Mark looked up and saw Brooke hanging onto the cliff face by one hand, her grip tenuous at best. Her other hand had hold of his right arm. The veins in her face and neck seemed to pop with the strain of holding onto him. He jerked suddenly as fear started to grip him.

"Mark, no!" Brooke cried out. "Don't do that or we'll fall."

He froze. "Fuck! Don't let me go."

"Reach up with your other hand and grab my arm."

Mark reached up and grabbed Brooke's wrist. It was wet and slippery.

"All right," she continued, her voice raised over the sound of the rushing water. "Reach over to the cliff face and put your hand into the crack. Do you see it?"

Mark looked at the granite wall facing him. It was wet and looked greasy. He let go with one hand and reached out, his fingertips falling painfully short. He tried to reach further and succeeded in scraping the hard surface with his fingernails.

"I can't reach it, Brooke."

"Try, Mark."

Mark reached out again, grunting with the exertion. Still though his efforts fell painfully short. "I can't do it," he cried out, his voice was edged with anger. His next words confirmed Brooke's fears. "Let me go, Brooke. Save yourself."

"If I hear you say that again, Mark Butler, I will let you go. Now shut up and do what I say."

He looked at her face. The excruciating pain of hanging on was gone, replaced by her own anger. He nodded, his face wet from the spray of water that rushed past.

"I'm going to swing you. When you get close to the cliff face get hold of that crack. You should be able to get your feet onto that thin ledge below it after that. You ready?"

"Do it."

"We'll only get one shot at this. Make it count."

Brooke started the swing. The muscles in her shoulder and back bunched and then released as she began the motion. Mark felt himself move, not much at first but after a few more seconds Brooke had him closer to the granite face. He reached out, stretched to the limit. His fingers touched the rough surface and then they slipped into the opening in the rockface.

His face lit up with relief as he realized he'd made it. But relief turned to terror as above him he heard Brooke scream as she lost her grip on the rock wall and started to plummet downward into oblivion.

———

Mark felt as though his right shoulder had been wrenched from its socket with the sudden jolt of Brooke's weight. His fingers dug viciously into her wrist, and he thought for a moment that he felt bones grind together. In the crack above, his left hand stuck fast, the only thing stopping them from plummeting earthward. Mark ground his teeth together in pain. He looked down at Brooke as she hung there. "You want to do something or just hang around? This could end a great relationship, you know."

"Just shut up," she shouted up at him.

Reaching out, Brooke managed to get a hold on the wall. She pulled herself across and found a foothold. Now free of her weight, Mark placed his feet on the narrow ledge she told him about before she fell.

Below him, Brooke climbed up and stopped beside him. "What now?" he asked her.

She looked to her left. "That way."

"I can't climb over there."

"You want to get off this cliff face, you'll have to. A thousand feet down, or a hundred feet to the left. You choose."

"Why do you suppose the tunnel came out here?" he asked her.

Brooke gave him a weird look. "Man, you ask some stupid questions at times."

"Sorry."

"Start climbing."

A thought came to him. "What happened to Greg?"

Brooke's face hardened. "He's gone."

"Are you sure?"

"Yes, I'm sure, blast your eyes. Now move. And get rid of that pack."

Mark's eyes widened. "No. The eggs."

"Fine, let's go."

They traversed the cliff face with Brooke guiding him all the way. By the time they reached the ledge Mark was exhausted. The rock shelf was wide enough for them to sit on, so they sat with their backs against the hard wall. To their right the water had slowed to a trickle as the spring sump had completely drained. Mark said, "It's a great view."

Brooke nodded. "It is."

"What do we do now?"

"We wait for someone to find us."

"I hope it's soon," Mark said. "I'm hungry."

Brooke burst out laughing. "Only you could think of food at a time like this."

She reached out and put her arm around him. She pulled him close, and he rested his head on her shoulder. Brooke rested her head on his. "I'm glad I'm stuck here with you."

"Really?" he asked surprised.

"Sure. If you say something to annoy me, I can push you off."

"Hmm, I never thought of that."

22

THE END OF THE BEGINNING

Berlin Germany, 1 Week Later

The Faberge Eggs sat on Schmidt's desk waiting to be picked up and stored in a vault until they would be sent back to their owners. Mark still looked upon them in awe as he stood with Brooke and Isabella listening to their benefactor. "They will be shipped to the location today. Molly and Werner are trying to trace the owners as we speak. You did a great job saving these. I'm very proud of your accomplishment."

Mark was still disappointed about losing the rest. "I know it's good, but we were so close. I saw—we saw part of the Amber Room with our own eyes."

"And you will see it again, Mister Butler. Of that, I'm sure. Kurt Stuber and his entourage can't hide forever. In fact, I'm not sure they want to. They're out there somewhere as we speak doing the same things we are."

"They're just not much good at it," Mark said.

Schmidt gave him a wry smile. "No, they're not. We make a good team, don't we?"

Mark nodded. "The best."

Brooke asked, "Are we sure he is Heinrich Wolfsjunge?"

"That is almost a certainty."

"Does Interpol have any idea where they might be?"

"No."

Mark shook his head.

Isabella took his arm. "Come on, I'll buy you a drink."

He looked at her and smiled. "Are we finished, sir?"

Schmidt nodded. "Yes, go and enjoy yourself."

The door to the office closed and Brooke looked at her boss. "Is everything prepared for Greg's funeral service?"

"Yes. His family will be attending as well."

Brooke nodded. "I think he'd like that."

"How did Mark do?"

"He did well. I think he'll fit right in."

"I'm pleased. However, I need you to do something for me."

"Sure."

Schmidt reached into his top drawer and took out a file. "I would like you to do a background check on this man. I'll be asking him to join our team in Greg's place."

Brooke frowned. "Don't you normally do that?"

"Not this time. Look what happened with Greg."

"You've done pretty well with the team you've put together, Johann. Don't begin to doubt yourself now. You did the same with Greg. Stuber got to him after you employed him."

"You're right but could you do it anyway, please? Get Mark to help, seeing as you're training him."

"All right."

"Thank you."

Brooke started towards the door, but Schmidt stopped her. "One more thing. After we've tidied things up and Greg is laid to rest, we're leaving on another search."

"Where to this time?"

"Portugal."

"Portugal?"

"Yes. Molly has been doing some digging into another matter and she might have come up with something."

"It must be big if we're all going," Brooke observed.

"It is. Ever heard of The Bishop's lost treasure? I'll fill you all in before we leave."

"I'll let Mark know so he can get a start on it."

Schmidt nodded. "Do that. It might take his mind off other things."

"Good, I've found you," Brooke said to Mark as he and Isabella crossed her path in one of the many corridors of the Foundation. "I just wanted to give you a heads up. We'll be leaving for Portugal within the week."

"What's in Portugal?"

"Something about a Bishop's treasure."

Excitement appeared on Isabella's face. "Wow, this is something. I knew Molly was working on our next expedition, but I didn't know what it would be."

Mark frowned. "I think I remember something about this. Pirates in the fourteenth century."

"That's it. Looks like you'll have a lot of reading to do before we leave."

"Good grief," Mark moaned.

"Have fun with that," Isabella said.

"It's all right," Brooke said. "I'll help him."

Mark smiled. "See, I knew you cared."

"Get away from me before I shoot you."

Brooke watched them walk away along the corridor, a smile on her lips. She knew he was right. She did care about him. In fact, she cared about them all. They were her family.

———

Somewhere in Southern Europe

"The last of the trucks have been unloaded," Anika said.

Stuber smiled. It was manufactured more out of relief than satisfaction. "Good. Once it is gone, we can seal it up."

"There was something else," she said.

"What?"

"Brooke Reynolds and Mark Butler escaped the mine."

Stuber turned and stared at her. "How?"

"I'm not sure. Would you like me to do something about it?"

"No. Their time will come. One day."

"It may be sooner than you think."

"Really?"

Anika nodded. "It would seem that they have been looking into something else."

Stuber's mood picked up even further. "Do tell."

"There was mention of a Bishop's Treasure."

The smile on Stuber's face widened. "Well, well, well. It would seem that the game is still afoot. Keep me appraised. As soon as they move, I want to know about it."

"Yes, sir."

"Was there something else?""

"Yes, sir. They've started on the room."

A broad grin split Stuber's face. "Good. Show me."

IF YOU LIKED THIS, YOU MAY ALSO ENJOY: TALON!
TALON SERIES BOOK ONE

The team nobody wants, but everybody fears …

When the British government approaches the Global Corporation about stemming the flow of human trafficking across the globe, Hank Jones turns to Mary Thurston to form a team right for the job. What she pieces together is a group of misfits—no longer wanted by anyone else—with talent to burn.

Led by disgraced German Intelligence officer Anja Meyer and SAS reject Jacob Hawk, the team is autonomous, utilizing the full force of the Global Corporation and its resources, as they track across different continents in pursuit of their elusive foe—a worldwide phenomenon called Medusa.

AVAILABLE NOW

ABOUT THE AUTHOR

A relative newcomer to the world of writing, Brent Towns self-published his first book, a western, in 2015. *Last Stand in Sanctuary* took him two years to write. His first hardcover book, a Black Horse Western, was published the following year.

Since then, he has written 26 western stories, including some in collaboration with British western author, Ben Bridges.

Also, he has written the novelization to the upcoming 2019 movie from One-Eyed Horse Productions, titled, *Bill Tilghman and the Outlaws*. Not bad for an Australian author, he thinks.

Brent Towns has also scripted three Commando Comics with another two to come.

He says, "The obvious next step for me was to venture into the world of men's action/adventure/thriller stories. Thus, Team Reaper was born."

A country town in Queensland, Australia, is where Brent lives with his wife and son.

In the past, he worked as a seaweed factory worker, a knife-hand in an abattoir, mowed lawns and tidied gardens, worked in caravan parks, and worked in the hire industry. And now, as well as writing books, Brent is a home tutor for his son doing distance education.

Brent's love of reading used to take over his life, now it's writing that does that; often sitting up until the small hours, bashing away at his tortured keyboard where he loses himself in the world of fiction.

CPSIA information can be obtained
at www.ICGtesting.com
Printed in the USA
LVHW041652280222
712228LV00013B/639